STREET OF STORYTELLERS

Doug Wilhelm

Rootstock Publishing

An imprint of Multicultural Media

Rootstock Publishing

Published by Rootstock Publishing
An imprint of Multicultural Media
Montpelier, Vermont
rootstockpublishing.com

Learn more at dougwilhelm.com

Library of Congress Control Number: 2018968619

ISBN-13: 978-1-5786901-6-9 (Rootstock Publishing)

Printed in the USA

PRAISE FOR STREET OF STORYTELLERS

"Street of Storytellers is a storytelling delight, following the journey of a teenage American into the teeming bazaars of Pakistan and a world of musicians, refugees, scholars and the religious fanatics who will become the followers of Osama bin Laden. The story is rich in detail and suspense. Young Luke, resentful of his father's research project and unwilling to learn about the culture around him, ends up learning more than he could ever have expected."

> – David Moats, author of *Civil Wars*
> and winner of the Pulitzer Prize

"Street of Storytellers is an ingeniously written tale about a young American's search for truth, love and meaning in an enchanting and sometimes violent world. Set in Peshawar, Pakistan, this exciting thriller is a marvelous portrayal of a society caught in the conflict between religious extremists and Sufi mystics, intolerance and freedom of expression, and the forces of hate and redemption through love."

> – Ali Asani, Professor of Indo-Muslim
> Cultures, Harvard University

"Street of Storytellers is a vivid and layered novel of family angst, clashing cultures, navigating friendships, first love, and wisdom versus extremism amid frightening political and religious tensions in 1984 Pakistan — as told by Luke, a 15 year old American who did not want to be there. Wilhelm skillfully weaves history into dramatic fiction that is both a personal story and a perspective on world events today."

> – Deborah Rodriguez, author of
> *Kabul Beauty School* and
> *The Little Coffee Shop of Kabul*

To the Community of the four quarters

Inscription found in a ruin of ancient Gandhara

ALSO BY DOUG WILHELM

Treasure Town

The Prince of Denial

True Shoes

Falling

The Revealers

Alexander the Great: Master of the Ancient World

Choose Your Own Adventure books

Snake Invasion

Curse of the Pirate Mist

The Underground Railroad

The Gold Medal Secret

Shadow of the Swastika

Gunfire at Gettysburg

Search the Amazon!

The Secret of Mystery Hill

Scene of the Crime

The Forgotten Planet

CONTENTS

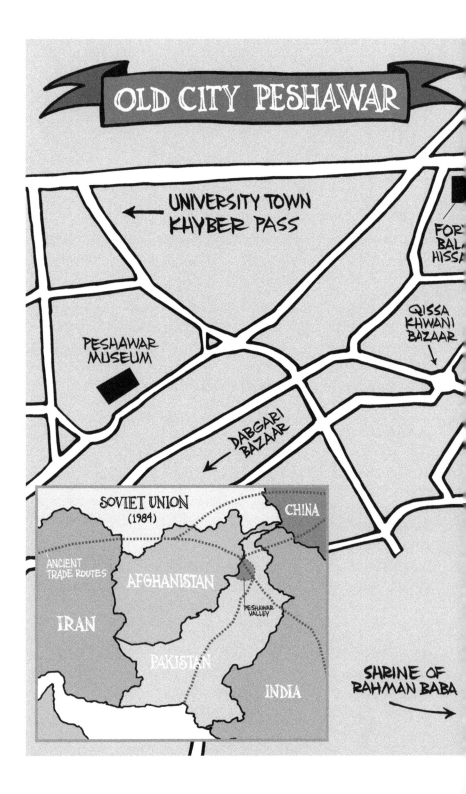

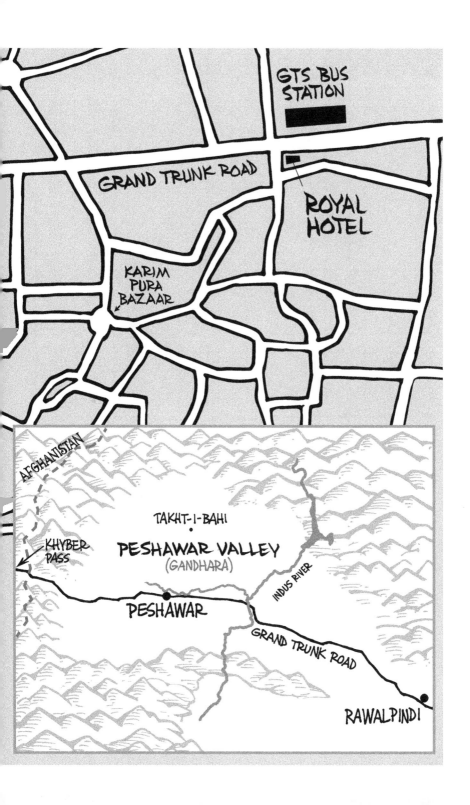

PART ONE

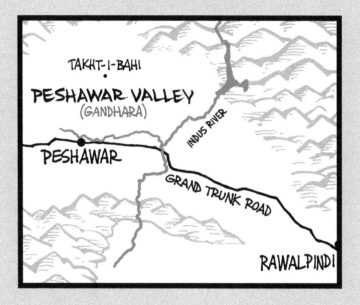

1.

Glory

Early evening of Monday, December 17, 1984
Peshawar, capital of the North-West Frontier Province
Pakistan

MY DAD GOT US SEPARATE ROOMS. (I'd have thrown a fit if he hadn't.) We were on the second floor of the hotel. My room was simple and narrow, with light blue walls and a window at the end that had wooden shutters, closed.

There was a bed, a dresser, a wooden desk and a chair. Out of my backpack I took my new, black-and-red Walkman cassette player and silver Toshiba headphones, early Christmas presents from my mom. I set them on the desk beside the red cassette case, size of a kid's lunchbox, with my twelve best tapes inside. I looked around the room—it seemed clean, which was a relief—and thought, *Okay. I can stay in here the whole vacation if I have to.*

Okay.

Because I had decided something. My dad had me over Christmas vacation, it said so in the divorce, so he could force me to fly with him halfway around the world to this weird place—but he couldn't make me *do* anything here if I didn't want to. What could he do, send me home? He had zero leverage at this point. So I had decided: I would not go anywhere, or do or see or learn anything, that had anything to do with the Great Goddamn Project.

He wanted me to understand, but I already understood. My dad's obsession with his project had wrecked my family. I would have nothing to do with it.

He didn't know this yet. But he would find out.

The Great Goddamn Project, or G.G. Project for short, was what my mom started calling it after my dad had been so obsessed for so long with working on his book about some lost civilization over here that my mom finally gave up on the marriage and moved out. Now we lived in a little apartment, her and me, except for every other weekend, when I had to hang around our old house where my dad kept on typing and typing behind the locked door of his home office, barely even aware I was there.

And now?

Now this.

There was a door between my room and his. Stuck in it was a big old-fashioned key. I went over and turned the key; the door locked with a *thunk*. I pulled hard but it held solid. I stood there and smiled.

Guess what, Dad?

The lock's on my side now.

Traffic whirled crazily, I mean *crazily,* out front of the Royal Hotel around an intersection that had a white concrete pedestal in the middle. On it stood a cop, wearing white gloves and waving helplessly at the chaos all around him—a honking, dodging, plunging whirl of cars, scooters, motorbikes, buses, painted-up trucks and skinny guys in pajamas risking death on black bicycles. A taxi pulled up, a tan Toyota. We got in it to go see the Shaheens.

Turning onto a busy avenue that my dad said was the Grand Trunk Road, we passed the Old City on the left, and the massive fort I'd seen when we came this way from the train station an hour ago. We made a right turn into a neighborhood that looked fairly regular, except each house had a high, solid wall all around it. Like each home was its own little fort.

"I need you to understand something," my dad said. "You think you know the Shaheens, and I'm not saying you don't—but we're in their country now. We're going to a Pashtun home."

"So?"

"Well, believe it or not, the fact that the women of the family will sit with us, eat with us, is very unusual here. I mean *very* unusual. In most Pashtun homes the women prepare food and tea, but they are not to be seen by non-family visitors. If you ask a Pashtun man about his family, most won't mention females at all."

I made a sound like I didn't believe that. Which I didn't.

"I know this sounds strange, but it's true," he said. "The Shaheens have lived in America, and they're modern, educated people—but they're still Pashtun. Don't try to hug Mrs. Shaheen or Danisha when we say hi."

"God, Dad. I'm not a hugger." Did he know *any*thing about me?

"And don't try to help them, okay? Don't even give them your glass when it's empty. The women will serve us, they'll do the work. That's their culture. All right?"

I shrugged again. "Whatever."

"I'm serious, Luke."

"*Okay.*"

The taxi pulled up at one of the house-forts, where a solid metal gate blocked the driveway. From a booth by the gate stepped a little white-bearded man. As he leaned into the window and spoke to the driver, I saw that his beard was bow-tied—it was knotted beneath his chin in a little neat bow. He peered at us, nodded, and went to open the gate.

The short driveway led to a squarish, pale yellow house. There was an orange tree in the yard, and a front porch screened with green vines. Down the porch steps burst the male Shaheens—first Rasheed, who was taller than when I'd seen him last and was trying to grow a beard, then Professor Shaheen, balding and grinning, his arms open wide.

"Welcome! Richard, Richard, it's fantastic—here you are!" Professor Shaheen said, embracing my dad. "And Luke. Why Luke, you've really grown."

"Hey, bro!" Rasheed shook my hand in both of his, then wrapped me in a quick hug. We stood back and studied each other.

Rashi was two years older than me. During the year that his family lived in our town, when his dad was a visiting professor at the college where my dad teaches, Rashi had been the outsider who talked a little loud, tried a little too hard to impress the cool guys. He was kind of awkward but I liked him okay. We were on the same soccer team; that was two years ago. Now he was seventeen, and he seemed awkward in some new way.

His hair was shaggy, he had the not-too-impressive beard, and he wore this long thing like an old-fashioned nightshirt of thick rough cloth. It had thin stripes and a hood pushed back. It didn't look like anything I had so far seen people wearing around here. I wondered who Rashi was trying to impress these days.

His mom and sister stood on the porch, in vine-shadowed dimness. They were both wearing those pajama-type outfits, though theirs were nicer than the ones I saw guys wearing in the streets. Professor Shaheen was dressed like a professor, with a tweedy old sport jacket. He said, "Richard and Luke, you remember my wife, Zari. And Danisha."

When I had seen Danisha last, she was a skinny kid who would tease Rashi in a sly way, and sometimes me too. As we came up the steps now, she stood in the shadows with her long hair falling dark and shiny from a silky headscarf, her eyes bright in a way that made my foot catch on a stair and I almost fell on my face.

Dani smiled. "Welcome, Professor," she said to my dad. "Hello, Luke."

"Uh...hi."

Then Rashi smacked me on the back and pushed me past his sister, through the front door into his house.

Before dinner we sat in the living room while Dani and her mom worked in the kitchen. When Mrs. Shaheen brought out a platter of snacks, I saw she'd put on a baseball cap. A Yankees cap.

"Whoa," I said. "I remember that hat."

"I thought you would!" She touched it, smiled. "Here I follow the cricket. But I miss baseball."

"Did you *watch* baseball?"

"I did! I had a lot of time at home, in Saratoga."

I said to Rashi, "That was your hat, right? I remember when you got it."

He shrugged. "Sports are for children," he said. His mom tugged the Yankees cap tighter on her head as she turned away.

The snacks were little dumplings with spiced meat inside. I ate a couple, they weren't too bad. There was also a bowl of pink and white candy; I bit into one and it had an almond inside. Dani came in with a tray of small bottles of Coke. When she set it down I was looking at her, but she didn't look up.

For dinner we had steak with mushroom gravy, mashed potatoes and green beans.

"Why, it's an all-American dinner! Very nice," Professor Shaheen said from the head of the table.

"I'd have thought you would prepare our traditional food," Rasheed said as his mom and sister sat down.

"I want you to feel comfortable your first night here," Mrs. Shaheen told us. She'd taken off the hat and put on a headscarf. "I hope your hotel rooms are acceptable."

"Mother! Don't speak of personal things," Rashi said. But she ignored him.

"They're great," my dad said. "At least mine is."

"Luke," she asked, "your room—is it all right?"

"Yeah. I mean yes. I kind of like it."

"Even so, there are nicer places in Peshawar."

"Sure, but the Royal is home," my dad said. "I've always stayed there, and it's right on the edge of the Old City. Luke'll see something of the real Peshawar."

"The *real* Peshawar is not in any hotel," Rashi said. His mom and dad glanced at him, in kind of a worried way.

"Well, sure," my dad said. "I'd like him to see a bit of the bazaars. And, of course, the ruins. The museum."

"Of course," Professor Shaheen said. "Our work."

"Bet you can't wait for *that*," Rashi, next to me, murmured in my ear. I shook my head, rolled my eyes. He saw that, and his eyebrows lifted.

"Rasheed," his mother warned.

"Well, maybe he doesn't want to do that. Maybe he'd rather see what's *really* going on here."

"How would you know?" Danisha asked. "*You* just pretend."

He reddened. She smiled.

"Danisha, please don't tease your brother," Mrs. Shaheen said. "They do this all the time," she told my dad. "You are so lucky to have only one."

"Uh…yeah," he said. "Rasheed, is that a *djellaba*?"

"Yes, sir," Rashi said, looking down at his robe.

"You don't see many of those around here."

"It's from Morocco. A brother from there gave it to me."

"Ah." My dad turned to me and said, "Morocco is in North Africa. Also a Muslim country."

"Okay, Dad."

"It's his costume," Dani told us innocently. "Can you guess what he's trying to be?"

I said, "A hippie?"

"No!" Her laugh was music. "A companion of our Holy Prophet Muhammad."

"Peace be upon him," Rashi added quickly.

"My brother thinks he can live in the past."

"It's not past—it's our *future*."

"You see, he's confused," Dani said. "He thinks we can live as if we're in some desert in Arabia, fourteen centuries ago."

"There is no time and place in the truth," Rashi said.

"What does that even mean?"

"*You* wouldn't know."

"Enough, you two," their mom said. "Honestly."

But Dani didn't stop. "My brother wishes to join the rebels, to be a holy warrior," she said to my dad. "He is full of wishes."

"They are *heroes*," Rashi declared, and he glared around at everyone.

"They are very brave," his father agreed quickly, and cleared his throat. "I'm so glad you're here—both of you," he said to my dad and me. "Peshawar"—he pronounced it *PeshOWur*—"is…interesting just now."

"Don't sugarcoat it! We're in a tight spot," Mrs. Shaheen told my dad. "We have Afghan refugees by the tens of thousands camped outside our city. The general who has seized power in Pakistan is a killer with cobra eyes—and he's giving so much power to the *mullahs* who want women and girls to all live hidden in our homes. Plus we are the staging ground for this horrible war."

"This *holy* war," Rashi said.

"Nothing is holy *about* it," she snapped. I could see heat rise in Rashi's face.

"How much longer do you think it'll go on?" my dad asked the Shaheens. To me he said, "We're just half an hour from the Afghanistan border. The Soviet Union has invaded the country over there."

"I know that, Dad."

"People said the fighting wouldn't last a month—but it has been five years," Mrs. Shaheen said. "Peshawar is stocked with guns and bombs. Afghans come over the border mountains wearing blankets and plastic sandals, pick up rifles and grenades and ammunition, then go back to be slaughtered by Russian boys in helicopter gunships. Where is the glory in that?"

"God protects the *mujahideen*," Rashi declared. "Bullets do not touch them. And when they go to paradise, they go with joy. Birds burst into song to welcome them."

"Of course they do," Dani said. I thought he might hit her.

"Rasheed, we all believe the Afghans' cause is noble," Professor Shaheen said. "But over there a proud old country is being destroyed, its best men murdered or tossed in dungeons—families are shattered, and *we* are swamped in the wreckage. How can such a catastrophe be heroic?"

"Because holy warriors give their lives to God!" Rashi almost shouted. "You *say* you're a historian—can't you see Peshawar is the anvil of history? *Our* history!"

Professor Shaheen glanced my way. "An anvil is a blacksmith's tool," he explained.

"That's right," said Rashi. "He heats metal until it's red-hot, then he hammers it on his anvil into something new. That's how a *sword* is forged."

"Oh yes," Dani said innocently. "It's all a very big forgery."

Rashi spun to his dad: "You cannot permit her to speak that way!"

"Address your father with respect," his mother warned.

"But why? In his own home he has no authority! He's too busy worshipping old stones."

"Rasheed, that's enough," his father said. He raised his Coke. "To your return, Richard. To our work."

"May you finish it at last," his wife said.

I kind of snorted. Everyone but Rashi and me raised their glasses.

"Good work takes time," Professor Shaheen said soothingly. "Still, it hasn't been easy for our families. We should be toasting *you*."

There was an awkward silence. Rashi was looking at me. "Hey," he said—"remember when we were Chargers?"

"Yeah, the soccer team. We were bad!"

The others laughed, and the grown-ups started talking again. Rashi leaned in close.

"I think we're on the same team again," he said, very low.

"What do you mean?"

He glanced around, then whispered, "I *hate* what they're doing. This cursed work. You too?"

"*Oh* yeah."

"Truly?"

"You have no idea."

He nodded. "Then you're with us."

"With who?"

"You'll see."

"*Rasheed,*" his mother said sharply. "What are you whispering about?"

He sat up straight. "I was saying there's more to Peshawar than old rocks," he said.

"They are more than rocks," Professor Shaheen said gently.

"Yes—they're idols. *Kafir* idols."

His mom stood up fast. "Rasheed Shaheen, leave this table! Go to your room. We will call you for dessert. Later."

Rashi shrugged, and stood. "Come visit," he said to me. "If you get *bored.*"

Then he strode in his stripey shirt out of the room.

Everyone seemed uncomfortable.

"I'm sorry you had to hear that," Mrs. Shaheen said to my dad. "It's hateful talk."

"What does it mean?" I asked. "Kafir?"

Nobody would look at me.

"It means an unbeliever," Dani said finally, looking down.

"Well...what's so bad about that?"

Again there was quiet. Professor Shaheen cleared his throat.

"In Muslim society," he told me, "to call someone this is not such a nice thing. I do apologize," he said to my dad.

"It's all right," my dad answered quickly. But I wasn't sure it was.

Dani said softly, shaking her head, "He really believes these sermons, this stuff about birds and paradise. It's like a song with no music."

"Oh, I got a new Walkman for Christmas!" I said—and the

grown-ups laughed again. "And I brought *Thriller,*" I told her, under the laughter.

Dani's eyes opened wide. She had sent a postcard, asking me to bring her a cassette of Michael Jackson's album. It wasn't my favorite, but I was happy to get it for her. I was all about the music.

The adults started talking again, and Dani looked at me. Her eyes were blue—not light blue, but kind of deep. I hadn't remembered how blue they were.

Then she stood and started gathering up the plates.

"Who is he involved with?" my dad asked, a little later. Dani and her mom had gone back into the kitchen.

"It's a group of foreigners," Professor Shaheen said. "Mostly they're Arabs, from Egypt and Saudi Arabia—idealistic young men who've come to join the rebels, to fight the Soviets. A guesthouse has been opened for them, here in University Town." Turning to me, he said, "That's this neighborhood."

My dad asked, "Is it a big group?"

"Well, it has been small, but just lately more are coming. They're drawn here by a popular preacher, Abdullah Azzam, a Palestinian extremist who's been living in Peshawar. Cassettes of his talks are all over the city. Now a rich Saudi fellow has come to join the cause, and he's bankrolling the welcome center. He'll pay the airfare for any young man who wants to fly here, from any Muslim country, to join the cause."

"Wow," my dad said.

"Yes, it's a bit scary. Azzam glorifies the violence so much. The Afghans' fight to throw the Russians out of their country is a bloody nightmare, and this man spins tales about the glory of dying for God. How would you feel if your son started to believe that?"

"I'd be terrified."

Professor Shaheen nodded. "Many of these boys come from countries like ours, with great poverty, harsh governments and little hope of making a useful life—and now this sheikh offers them a mission that feels glorious. My son thinks he has found *the answer.* And I find it harder and harder to sleep at night."

"Who's the guy that's spending so much?"

"Oh, he's from some super-rich Saudi family. The newest rumor is that he has begun telling these boys—mind you, they haven't even fought in a battle yet—that they have an even bigger mission, against what he says are Islam's enemies. Some larger *jihad.*"

"Like what?"

"I don't know. Rasheed has become secretive. He used to tell me everything, but…well, you know. He's a teenager."

My dad nodded, like he understood. "What's his name? The rich guy?"

"I'll think of it. Meanwhile, my friend, I wonder if I might chat with *your* boy for a moment? Just the two of us."

My dad looked at me like he'd forgotten I was here. He shrugged.

"Why not? You can't do worse than I've been doing. I'll step onto the porch. Take in this mild evening."

When he was gone, Professor Shaheen held out his hand. "My friend, welcome to Peshawar."

I shook it. "Thanks. I guess."

He laughed. "Have you got mixed feelings? I can hardly blame you—I'm afraid our family is a fair sampling of what's happening here. Our little city at the crossroads of old empires is turning into …well, I don't even know. But it worries me a bit, that your father has brought you here. I do understand why," he added quickly. "It's terribly important to Richard that you see what we're doing. He so much wants you to understand."

I didn't answer.

"But one reason why your dad is such a fine historian is that he focuses so completely on his—well, his area of interest. Sometimes he may not spot the bigger picture. I say this with all respect."

"No problem," I said. "I've kind of noticed."

He chuckled. "I expect you have. But tonight, if I may, I would like to offer you one small lesson. I am always the professor, you see—and this may be the most important thing I can give you right now."

I listened. What was this?

"You're in a very different place," he said.

"I guess."

"Sure, it's obvious—but not in *every* way. There are many layers of what's going on in Peshawar. We have marvelous folks—faithful people, good, strong and wise people—and we have...other kinds.

"So here you are, a young American," he said. "People will want to meet you, talk with you. How can you spot the ones you can trust? How do you tell the false from the true?"

I didn't answer. I didn't know.

"Trust everyone, and you could get into a sticky situation," he said. "But trust no one and you won't learn anything—or make any friends! And there *are* friends here. You've already got us."

I thought about Rashi, who'd said we were on the same team. And Dani.

Professor Shaheen leaned forward. "Trust your first impressions," he said.

"Huh?"

"It's simple. When you meet someone, your very first sense of them is the voice of your intuition—and it will be true. If you meet someone and get a funny feeling, an uncomfortable sense, then trust it. And don't trust that person."

"Okay..."

This was kind of cool, actually. Like secret knowledge.

"You are American, so people will think you are rich, and maybe important. They may be good at talking, at drawing you in—but stay with your first impressions. If you meet someone and have a good sense, if your feeling says this is a true person—well, that could be the friend you need. And we all need friends, don't we?"

I nodded. Sure.

"Of course, you won't be wandering around by yourself," he said, "but your father and I will often be working, and this is what concerns me. Even at your hotel, you should be somewhat careful. The Royal is a crossroads, just like this city. All sorts of people go in and out."

The professor tapped his chest. "At a time and place like this, we must stay alert, and listen to the whisper within. It will tell you."

My dad blundered back in, saw us talking closely. "Oh. Am I back too soon?"

"Not at all! My little lecture has just concluded," Professor Shaheen said, and he winked at me. "By the way," he said to my dad, "I thought of that fellow's name."

"Who?"

"The Saudi guy. With the money and the bigger jihad."

"Oh, right. What is it?"

"Bin Laden," Professor Shaheen said. "Osama bin Laden, I think."

After we got back to the hotel and went into our rooms, I wanted to stay up—to stay up late and look out the window and listen to my best music. I wanted to hear the songs that swept you up inside.

I wanted her to *see* me.

I was lit up with remembering the light in her face, how she had teased her brother and how she had looked, and I remembered her eyes. Deep blue. I opened the shutters and stared at the alley below, where there were cobblestones and one lonely streetlamp. I stood there, listening to my music, for a long time.

While I was looking, a woman hustled along the alley. She was wrapped up in some all-hiding cloak, and she moved quickly, like a ghost in the lamplight. Like she was scared or something.

2.

Music

I WOKE UP TOO EARLY, to the racket of a typewriter next door.

*Whack whack pock pock **ping**!*

I yanked the pillow over my head. He was *already* working.

*Pock pock **ping**!*

At home I'd hear that clacketing and pinging late at night and way too early, like now, every single morning. It meant my dad was stealing every hour he could, outside his teaching schedule at the college—never mind about his family, what was that? or anything else—to work on his stupid book.

Ping!

"Aw, *man...*"

I groped for the Walkman, pulled on the 'phones and jabbed Play. Bob Marley surged in my ears. In the dim light I looked at the door between our rooms. Still locked.

Today I would be locking more than that door.

"You must learn to order tea like a Pashtun," Professor Shaheen said to me with a big grin.

He'd shown up at breakfast in the hotel dining room lugging an overstuffed shoulder bag. When he set it on our table and zipped it open, I saw the bag was loaded with file folders, each one crammed full of papers and photos.

I realized what this meant.

The Great Goddamn Project had been living in two places, the Shaheens' house in Peshawar and ours in Saratoga, but now it had all come here. All of it. My dad said it would be a big fancy book, full of photos and maps and whatever. So this meant the whole obsession would be nested—and worked on and fussed over, day and night—in my dad's room. Next to mine.

Great, I thought. *That's just great.*

"English-style tea, we call *chai,*" Professor Shaheen was saying. "That is black tea with milk and sugar. In the bazaar, it will come mixed. Here it will come with milk and sugar on the side."

"We had bazaar chai in the train station," my dad said. "In Rawalpindi, right, Luke? We came there from the airport."

"I know where it was, Dad."

"But *our* tea is green tea," Professor Shaheen went on. "We call it *qawa.* It's flavored with cardamom seeds. It's very nice."

I shrugged. "Okay."

He turned and said something in another language. A boy came up to our table. He looked about my age. His white waiter's jacket was clean.

"Good morning, sir," the kid said to Professor Shaheen.

"Good morning, Yusuf. How are you? How's your father?"

"We are well, sir. Thank you."

"Luke?" Professor Shaheen said to me. "Would you like to order something?"

At first I didn't get it—but then I did. He wanted me to learn.

"Um...what's it again?"

"Qawa."

"Right." To the boy I said, "Um...qawa?"

He nodded. "Sure." He turned to my dad. "Sir?"

"Chai, please."

The qawa when it came was clear, slightly green. It tasted soft and fresh.

"We put a little sugar in it, usually," Professor Shaheen said. (I put in a lot.) "In the bazaar, it will come to you sweet."

"What's the bazaar?"

"Ah! So many things. *The bazaar* can mean a district of the city—a neighborhood, a street where goods are sold. If you say 'in the bazaar' here, you mean within the Old City—anyplace, really, on its ancient streets where everything you can imagine is bought, sold or communicated."

He said to my dad, "Luke must see the Old City. It's the soul of Peshawar."

"Of course. But first, breakfast—and then the museum. That's today."

I didn't say anything. But I wasn't going to any museum.

I had a plain omelette (it sounded safe) and toast. My dad ate his scrambled eggs quickly. I ate slowly. Made myself take steady breaths.

My dad hopped up. "Let me stow this in the room before we go," he said, lifting the bag. "Oof—you weren't kidding!"

"Three years of work, my friend," said Professor Shaheen. "It's all there."

As my dad went up the stairs, Professor Shaheen turned to me. "I...hope I didn't frighten you last night," he said. "With my talk about this place."

"Huh? Oh...not really."

"Well, I hope not. I'm afraid I worried about this, rather late into the night."

"'Bout what?"

"Well, I don't want you to think we have become something other than a good family—the way you knew us," he said. "We still are. But all the tension in Peshawar, it's as if we've got the same in our house. There's the awful war next door, and these extremists grabbing for power across Pakistan, telling everyone that women should be shut away—and now Rasheed is mixed up with this new group. These young men from other countries who want to be warriors."

Electric heaters glowed red along the walls. As the white-jacketed boy brought breakfast to another table, Professor Shaheen leaned over ours. "I don't believe Rasheed means to harm anyone," he said. "He thinks he has found something to belong to—and he's a good boy, really. He cares so much."

I didn't know what to say. It was all pretty strange. We sat awkwardly until my dad came bustling back down, a smaller bag over his shoulder and a camera hanging from his neck. He looked like an excitable tourist.

"So, Luke!" he said. "This morning we'll be seeing the Peshawar Museum. We need to do a little more photography there."

"It's our treasure house," Professor Shaheen said. "You will be amazed."

I took a breath. It was time.

"Ummm...Mr. Shaheen?"

"*Professor* Shaheen," said my dad.

"Yeah, um, Professor? Could I talk with my dad for a minute? Not to be rude or anything."

"Not at all." He stood. "I'll arrange for a rickshaw."

As the professor went to the lobby, I said to my dad, "A *rickshaw*?"

"Yeah—a motor-scooter rickshaw. Every ride's an adventure," he said, and chuckled. "What's up?"

"Dad." I looked at the table.

"Spit it out, okay? We need to get going."

I shook my head. "Uh-uh."

"Huh?"

"You guys go. I'm not."

His forehead wrinkled. "Not what?"

"Not going. I'll stay here."

He shook his head. "Luke...we need to take you. To *show* you. I can't tell you how long I've wanted to do this."

"So go ahead. I'll be fine."

He peered at me. "I don't get it. You don't want to come?"

"I'm not going."

"Why not?"

"Because."

He peered closer. "Did your mother put you up to this?"

"What? *No.* Give me a break, Dad."

"But... I mean... why would you want to just hang around a hotel when we're in one of the most interesting places in the world?"

"Interesting to *you,* okay? Look, you made me come here— on my Christmas vacation. So fine, I'm here. But this is as far as I go."

He looked around. "This?"

"Yeah."

"Why?"

"Because it is." I looked at him, straight and level.

"But, I mean"—he was flustered, waving toward the outside— "it means a lot, you coming with us. I just... I need you to get it. I need you to *see.*"

"I can see fine. I'm not going."

His face tightened. "Yes, you are, Luke."

"No I'm not. Dad."

"I am not leaving you in this hotel all day!"

"What're you gonna do—ground me? Go ahead." I crossed my arms. "Or, hey! Send me *home.*"

I looked at the boy in the white jacket. Standing against the wall across the dining room, he nodded.

My dad staggered out to the lobby. I watched him talk to Professor Shaheen, gesturing and shrugging and shaking his head. The professor glanced at me, then said something. My dad turned to come back, but his friend touched his shoulder and said something more.

Now it was just Professor Shaheen coming back. He sat down. Studied me.

"I understand you've made a choice," he said.

I took a breath. "No offense or anything—I'm sure the museum is cool, if you like museums. I just…"

"You know, it's fine."

"Huh?"

"Your staying here. This is your holiday. And none of this was your idea, was it?"

My face got warm. "No."

"I understand." He looked down for a bit, then back up. "We Shaheens were terribly sorry to learn of the breakup of the Sands."

"Yeah," I mumbled.

"This has been hard for you. Do you think your parents will get back together?"

I shook my head.

"Why not?"

"My mom's got a boyfriend now. And my dad…" I shrugged.

"Perhaps you are blaming him—and perhaps he deserves it," he said. "But he also has lost a lot, can you see it? And bringing you here—it means so much to him. He wants to share our work, our mission, whatever we may call it, with his son. With you."

"But it's not *about* that—it's about you guys working," I said. "He'll be working the whole time. I'll be stuck in this hotel anyway —I *know* him. So, please, I mean…do your thing, or whatever. I'll be fine."

Professor Shaheen slowly shook his head. "I wonder what we have done," he said. "This valley holds an age-old story that is all but forgotten, and we have put so much into telling it to the world. But have we sacrificed our families to tell it? Is it you who must pay the price?"

He took a breath, and stood up. "If you'll excuse me, Luke, I will speak with your dad."

"Well…what'll you say?"

"That you have chosen to hang out." He smiled. "See? I did learn some American lingo." He pondered again. "Perhaps this afternoon you'd like to visit the family?"

"Your family?"

"Of course. Mrs. Shaheen will give you tea—I will call and let her know. How would that be, all right?"

"Well...sure." Would Dani be there?

"Let me have a chat with Richard," he said.

In the lobby, my dad listened to Professor Shaheen, occasionally glancing my way. Then they came back.

"Your father says this is okay. But he has one big concern," the professor said.

"I don't want you going anywhere—not alone," my dad said. "This isn't Saratoga."

"But...you just *said* you don't want me hanging around here!" It wasn't fair!

"I may have an answer," Professor Shaheen said. "Can you give me a moment?"

We stood by the table, silent and tense. The professor came back with the boy in the white jacket.

"Professor Sands, meet Yusuf Salif."

"Good morning, sir." The boy stood straight, held out his hand.

"Hello, Yusuf." They shook. "Nice to meet you."

"And you as well." The boy turned to me. "Hello," he said.

"Hey. I'm Luke."

We shook. He seemed pretty serious.

"Yusuf is someone I know," the professor said. "His father cooks here. They are from Kabul, the Afghan capital, and they have come through a great deal. Yusuf is trustworthy—and Luke, he would be pleased to accompany you to my home this afternoon." Turning to my dad, he added, "I can vouch for him."

My dad hesitated, studied us. Yusuf was about my height, with dark brown serious eyes.

"All right. We'll try it," my dad said. "But once you leave this hotel, except inside the Shaheens' house, neither of you boys leaves the other's sight. Is that understood?"

He looked at us. We nodded.

"Excellent! Then all is well," said Professor Shaheen. To Yusuf he added, in English, "This young man is a guest in your house." They said more, in a crackle-edged language, and they shook hands.

"We will see you later!" the professor said. He turned to go, but my dad just stood there, looking at me. His face was complicated, like he wasn't sure how to feel.

"It's okay," I said. "This is good."

After a couple of seconds, he nodded. He shook his head and sighed. Then, at last, he went.

I said to this kid, "I'm gonna hang out upstairs awhile. Okay?"

"Sure. After lunch, I am free."

I started to go, then turned back. "I've got music," I said.

A glimmer lit his face for just a second, then he was wary. "Good music?"

"Oh yes."

He looked at me closely. Then he nodded, and went back to work.

All morning I listened to Bob Marley, who was my absolute favorite. Half the cassettes in the red zippered case were Bob. After a while, when I opened my door to go to the bathroom down the hall, there was a tray right there on the floor. It had a white teacup and a small pot. I brought it in; the pot was full of sweetened qawa. I drank it listening to *Exodus*.

Around noon, I came downstairs. More men were at the tables. No women. Yusuf was bustling around. When he came over, I asked for a chicken sandwich.

"Sure."

"Was that you that brought tea? To my room?"

He nodded.

"Thanks—it was good. So…you still want to go? After this?"

"Of course. In one hour I will be finished. You can wait?"

I nodded, then put the 'phones on with the Bob and the Wailers' album *Burnin'*. Around me the men hunched over tables, talking seriously. It was like I was watching a movie, of a place that was pretty strange but had a cool soundtrack.

Out front a metal railing separated the sidewalk from the crazy intersection. "Get Up Stand Up," cranked up loud, gave this scene a pulsing rhythm as a truck painted all over with colored scenes came charging at a skinny guy pulling a heavy-loaded cart while a motorcyclist shot past like a circus clown, head down, pell-mell. In my ears the music mingled with the beeping blaring horns, then something made me look to the right.

Yusuf was leaning against the rail. He had on jeans and a T-shirt, like me. I took off my headphones and slipped them on his head.

His eyebrows shot up; he looked at me and whispered, "Bob*marli*."

I thought, *Huh!*

He listened for just a bit, then handed me the 'phones. He said, "You like Bobmarli?"

"I *love* Bob Marley. *You* like Bob Marley?"

He nodded firmly. But he didn't say anything.

"Um…hey," I said, "I brought some tapes! Do people listen to Bob here?"

He shrugged. "Music like this is difficult to get," he said. I felt like there was more, but he didn't say more. It was like he was contained in himself.

"Here," I said, and put the 'phones back on his head. He was nodding to the rhythm, the traffic surging a few feet away. Then he took the headphones off and handed them back.

"Thank you."

"Any time," I told him.

"Are you ready to go?"

"Um, yeah, but—I don't really know where this house is."

"I do. The professor told me."

"Oh, cool! Then I just need to go upstairs. Get some stuff."

"I will get a rickshaw," Yusuf said.

When I came back with the Michael Jackson tape for Dani, parked by the corner was a bizarre little vehicle. Its front was like a motor scooter with a big windshield, but the back was a squarish black cocoon, with plastic windows and a shiny red bench inside.

"*That's* a rickshaw?"

"Yes. Do you have these in the U.S.?"

"Oh God no."

The thing's side was painted with flowers, with swirly patterns and a mustached smiling guy like a movie star. The back had a cartoony war scene: jet fighters like birds, swooping down on a rocket launcher as it shot off a missile. Splash of red.

When we had squeezed ourselves inside on the bench, the driver shot across the intersection, blaring his tinny horn. Soon to the left I saw a haze over a jumble of rooftops.

"The Old City," Yusuf said over the blatting engine.

"I guess."

"You would like to go?"

"I don't know. Maybe?"

"If we just walk back from the hotel, we are in the bazaar," he said as we bumped, swayed and clattered along. "Maybe later we can go. With permission, of course."

"Sure, maybe. Hey, in the neighborhood where we're going, the houses have these high walls. And guards."

"Yes."

"But why? Is it that dangerous here?"

"No no, it is our custom. Pashtun people like to keep their home life private."

"Okay. So...you're Pashtun?"

"Sure. Almost everyone is—from Kabul in my country, in the mountains along the border, and here in this valley. All Pashtun people."

"Huh."

"It's okay. We like Americans."

"Yeah?"

"Of course. Your country is our friend, and we like your President Reagan. Very handsome."

"He *was* a movie star."

"Yes, and he has said that our great enemy, Russia, the Soviet Union, is an evil empire. They invaded my country. What he said is true."

"I remember he said that."

Yusuf nodded. "So we are on the same side."

I looked out at the honking, smoky craziness.

"Good to know," I said.

Outside the Shaheens', we unfolded ourselves like bugs from a cocoon. Yusuf paid the driver as the old guy with the bow-tied beard came out of the tiny guard's shed. He spoke with Yusuf, and they shook hands. The man opened the gate.

"You go," Yusuf said.

"Well...what about you?"

"I will wait here. With the *chokidar*."

He nodded to the old man, who stood very straight, as if he had long ago been a soldier.

3.

Brothers

"AH, LUKE, COME IN," Mrs. Shaheen said. "My husband said you would be coming. Rasheed is here."

"Hey, bro!" Rashi strode into the front hall, still wearing his stripey hooded thing.

"I, um, brought some music," I said, taking *Thriller* out of my backpack. "That Dani wanted."

Mrs. Shaheen glanced at Rasheed. He folded his arms, and she stiffened. "She will be home from school in an hour," she said. "You can give it to her then."

I put the cassette away. Rashi draped an arm over my shoulder and nodded at the backpack. "Leave that here," he said. "When men want to talk, they go to the cafe. Come. I know a good place."

He steered me out onto the porch. The door closed quietly behind us.

"A cafe?"

"Yes. Where men can talk."

"Well...okay. But I came with a guy."

"A guy?" He peered around. "Who?"

"He's a kid who works at my hotel—your dad knows him. My dad made us promise we'd stick together. For safety, or whatever."

"Where is he?"

"With the...with the..." I pointed to the closed gate.

"The chokidar?"

"Yeah."

Rashi called something, the gate opened, and the old guard appeared, with Yusuf behind him. Rashi strode up to him and there was a flurry of talking. They shook hands, but Yusuf didn't smile.

"Okay. He'll come with us," Rashi told me. "We can walk, no problem. It's just nearby."

Soon the orderly streets of University Town emerged onto a straight avenue. Rashi led us to a small cafe whose front was open to the street. It had just a few tables, all but one of them empty.

Weird music warbled from a cassette system on a shelf as I followed Rashi in. The only person here was a preppy-looking youngish man, who stood up smiling. I looked back for Yusuf, but he was out across the avenue, standing by a vendor's rickety stall, watching.

"Luke. Luke!"

"Huh?"

"Luke, my brother," Rasheed said. "This is Abu Amal. You can call him Amal. He is also my brother."

The guy called Amal held out his hand, and we shook. "Welcome!" he said. He had on a yellow polo shirt and expensive-looking jeans. His hair was carefully combed and he was handsome. Rasheed looked especially awkward, in his rough desert garment next to this country-club person.

"Please sit," Amal said, smiling and waving me to a chair. "You like tea? Coffee?"

"Uh, tea."

"Sure. Black tea. Nice and strong, right?"

"Okay."

Amal called out commandingly, and a sulky-looking skinny guy quickly brought a tray. It had a cup of milky tea in a chipped mug, and a plate of butter cookies.

"Have some. Please—they are for you," Amal said as he sat down across the little table. "You are smart to take tea. I am from

Saudi Arabia, so I must drink coffee. It is required!" He smiled. "But the coffee here, it's pure shit." He made a face like he'd bit a lemon. "Nescafé instant, very bad. In the U.S. you have good coffee."

"You've been to the U.S.?"

"Oh sure! I was a student at American University, in D.C. I liked it," Amal said. "You live in a college town, yes?" Rashi, beside him, nodded eagerly.

"I do, yeah. My dad teaches there."

"And you have come here because of some work he is doing."

"Yeah," I said, unhappily.

"You are not part of this work?"

"Oh God no. Not a fan."

"We *hate* the work," Rashi put in. "We both—"

"Brother." Amal held up his hand, and Rashi stopped.

Now Amal wrinkled his forehead, like he was trying to understand. "But your father has brought you here," he said. "On your holiday?"

"Yep."

"I think you are not so happy about this."

"Definitely not," I said.

Amal sat back, and shrugged. "It *is* a strange place, no? So noisy."

"Yeah! Where we're staying, it's crazy."

"Oh yes, so much traffic there. Much nicer to come to a quiet place, where you can talk with friends." He waved around at the empty cafe. "Here you are welcome! We are friends here. Like brothers, really." He smiled, poured more tea, waved at the cookies. "Please."

"Thanks." I ate another cookie. The weird music warbled. Amal looked like he was thinking. Then he leaned toward me.

"Forgive me, but…this work of your father's, that he has come here to do. Has it made difficulties for you?"

"Huh! My dad's so in love with it, it broke up my family. I get hauled around like luggage now."

He was concerned. "Luggage?"

"Yeah. Every other weekend, from my mom's apartment to my

dad's house where we used to live. And now here. It basically sucks."

I looked around. Yusuf was still out there. Watching.

"But this is your personal business, a family matter," Amal said. "We should not even speak of it."

"No, that's okay." It was kind of a relief, actually, to talk about it.

"Divorce is terrible," Rashi put in. "It's not *moral*." Amal looked his way, and he quieted.

Amal leaned over the table, and spoke more softly. "I think we should make you a promise, that we will not speak of this to anyone else." He looked at Rashi. "We agree, yes? This is a private thing. Just between us."

"Of course," said Rashi.

"But something like this should never happen," Amal said to me. "We all have families, we love our families."

"It's because of that book," Rashi said. "It's cursed! It's against—"

"Brother," Amal said mildly. He really did seem concerned. "So this *is* a problem," he said to me. "This work your father is doing, with the father of Abu Muiz."

"Who?"

"That's me," Rashi said. "It means *bestower of honor*."

"Why?"

"Why does it mean that?"

"No, why use a fake name?"

"It's not fake!" he said. "It's my *true* name."

"O…kay…" That was a little strange. Amal was looking at me searchingly.

"May I tell you something? This is a problem for us, too, this work." His hand circled us, all together. "We are brothers, in this way."

"Well, okay. But why?"

He shrugged. "Another time, we can talk about that. And we have promised—in this place, on our honor—not to speak of this with anyone else. We make this promise together." He looked around. "Yes?"

"Yes," Rashi said. Amal looked at me. I shrugged.

"Sure."

"Very good," he said. "We can talk again tomorrow, maybe—but please, have more tea. I will finish this terrible coffee, then I must go."

Amal drank, then he stood and offered his hand. We shook again.

"Now you have friends here," he said, and smiled. "You are welcome!"

As we walked back to his house, Rashi talked about his friends.

"They're from all over—all the Muslim countries," he said. "They come by plane, by train. To the Services Bureau."

"What's that?"

"It's a guesthouse. Right near our house, actually."

Rashi glanced over at Yusuf, then he stopped talking. Yusuf never said anything. When we got to the house, he stayed outside the gate as we went in.

On the porch, Rashi stopped and stood close. "We're on the same side, Luke," he assured me. "You'll understand more soon, don't worry."

I shrugged. "Okay." I was wondering if Dani was inside.

The tray Mrs. Shaheen brought into the living room had two cups and a teapot with red dragons on it, like from China. Behind her came Dani, carrying a tray stacked with cookies. She had on the long-tailed pajamas that most of the men around here seemed to be wearing—but hers were perfectly ironed, a pale blue top and cream-colored pants. Her headscarf was blue, too. Like her eyes.

"I...um...I brought you that music," I blurted.

"Did you really? *Thriller?*" she asked as she set the tray on the table. I nodded as Rashi sat watching. I turned to get the backpack and...Hey, where was my backpack? Did I leave it in the cafe? I looked around, confused.

Dani left the room; then she glided back in, smiling, my backpack dangling from her fingers.

"Are you missing something?"

"Oh…right," I said. "I remember."

She set it on the table. I zipped open the front pocket and handed her the tape.

Dani held *Thriller* to her heart. "Thank you *so* much."

"Oh sure."

"My friends and I are crazy for music," she said. "But nobody has *this*."

"It's enough," Rasheed said to his sister. "Now go."

Dani stiffened. "Actually, I think I will stay." She perched on a chair, picked up a vanilla-creme cookie. She nibbled a small piece, looking at her brother. "These are good," she said.

"Mother!" Rashi called out.

Mrs. Shaheen came to the door. "My son," she said, nodding at him. She asked me, "How is tea?"

"Oh, it's great. Thanks." I'd never drunk so much tea in my life. I'd never drunk *tea* in my life.

"It's time we men are left alone," Rashi said. "To talk."

"Is that so?" His mom smiled. "Do you have great things to talk about?"

"Maybe we do." Rashi glanced at me.

"Our brains are small for such matters," Dani said to her mother.

"Enough," Rashi said, but he wasn't looking at anyone. "It's enough."

"Is it?" Dani asked. "Are you the ruler of the house, then?"

"I will be. And then you will—"

"Until then, young man, you will show respect," his mother snapped. "I won't have this lording about. Do you understand me?"

Rashi stared at nothing.

"Yes."

"Yes what?"

"Yes, *Mor.*"

"Thank you," Mrs. Shaheen said, and she swept back into the kitchen.

Dani went out too—but then she came back, with a big silvery cassette player.

"Take that away!" Rashi said. But she set the machine on a table by the couch. She plugged it in, and clicked in the *Thriller* cassette.

"That music is trash," her brother growled.

"It's not *that* bad," I said. I wasn't a huge Michael Jackson fan, but still.

Dani hit Play, and the living room filled with "Wanna Be Startin' Somethin'"—first the electronic beat, then Michael. Dani perched on a chair and gazed pleasantly at her brother, who glared at the music machine.

4.

Catch a Fire

WHEN YOU FIRST FIND YOURSELF in a place like this that's *so* different, so much comes at you, so many impressions. I was pretty overwhelmed, and confused by the things that had happened today. On the ride back to the Royal, Yusuf and I were crammed in a rickshaw and I was staring out at the traffic when I saw something really strange.

Walking alongside the road were two figures covered completely in pale blue cloth, like they had on curtains with eye slits. Our driver honked. He turned, and I did also, to look at the figures as we passed.

I looked at Yusuf. He nodded. "Women," he said.

I sat back, baffled. Questions swirled in my head, like why had Rashi taken me to meet that guy? Amal had seemed okay—he was friendly, he was interested, and he'd been waiting for us. Why? And why had Yusuf stayed outside the cafe?

And could I avoid taking sides between Rashi and Dani? I didn't want to, but I was pretty sure Rashi wanted me to. I wasn't sure what Dani wanted—and then I saw those women, shuffling along all cloaked over like that. Now I could see the Royal Hotel up ahead, and I thought, *There's a lot I don't get about this place.*

A lot.

Then we were walking in the front door, and Yusuf had to go to work.

For dinner at the hotel I had the scrawniest chicken I had ever seen. I had to pick the meat out of it. The fries were sort of okay, but the ketchup was terrible; it was watery and didn't taste like ketchup at all. It didn't taste like anything. I felt homesick and sad.

"I understand you brought Danisha some music," my dad said.

"Well...how'd *you* hear that?"

He shrugged. "News travels fast in Peshawar. Listen, Luke, I have to tell you something. The Pashtun people—I admire a lot about them. They're absolutely real, and no one tells them what to do. They're like Americans in that way. But they are very different from us in their attitudes about women. About their women especially."

Picking at my chicken, I pretended not to listen.

"Part of it is the culture of Islam," he said. "Muslim women are generally considered to need protection, and there's a strong tradition of modesty in public, girls and women covering their heads and so forth. But Pashtuns enforce an almost complete separation of the sexes outside the home."

"Why do women wear those blue things? With the eye slits?"

"They're called *burqas*. Horrible things. And this is what I'm saying: Out in the street, women cannot show any part of themselves. In the home, the woman with seniority—like the mother, like Mrs. Shaheen—does have influence and importance. But the father, the head of the household, is always the final authority."

"Okay..."

"So this is something we have to be very careful about," he said. "What you and I would consider a normal friendship with Danisha, like you and she had back home, Pashtun men would see completely differently. You just have no idea."

"But we *know* the Shaheens. God, Dad."

"Yes, and they're a worldly family, but they're still Pashtun. This business of keeping women covered outside, and keeping their world separate and enclosed inside—Pashtun men are deadly serious about this. *Deadly* serious. Even a modern guy like Assad has to follow this, see, because the culture enforces it.

"You don't want to test this, Luke. If you did, the one who'd get hurt wouldn't be you. It would be her."

"Dad," I said, patiently. "What are you talking about?"

"It seems bizarre, I know—but here it's very real. This is Pashtun country, and the first law of their tradition is hospitality. If you are a Pashtun's guest, he will honor you, feed you, protect you. A Pashtun will never turn away a guest—that's the first law. But the *second* law, Luke, is revenge. And they mean it.

"A young, unmarried woman like Danisha is seen as carrying the honor of her family. After faith in God, the family's honor comes first. If Pashtun men feel a daughter or sister has dishonored the family, brought shame to it—which they believe she can do just by having friendly contact with a boy—then that girl can be in very big trouble."

"But... what could happen?"

"Well, forced marriage. Eventually, no matter what, a girl's parents and her family's elders will choose her husband—but that could happen in a sudden rush. She could be bundled off to the most available man, no matter who he is, however old or unsuitable.

"It can get worse, Luke. For an 'offense' that to you and me would seem perfectly normal—like being seen talking in public with a boy, even with no touching, and you must *never ever* touch an unmarried Pashtun girl—for this, girls are sometimes killed. By their own fathers and brothers."

"*Killed?*"

"I'm telling you, Luke. I'm not saying the Shaheens would do that—I know they wouldn't. But every household here is part of a big family network. All over Peshawar, Assad and Zari have aunts, uncles, cousins. If Danisha were seen as having shamed those folks, the pressure on Assad and his son to do something could be intense. Or someone else in the network could do something.

"Don't create that situation, Luke. You can still be *friends* with Dani—but be very, very careful how you interact with her. Only inside the home, and always with Rasheed or a parent there. Right there always, brief conversations with supervision. When I say the daughter holds the family's honor, I mean they believe she holds it in her body. That's how they see it. So no close contact, and no touching absolutely ever. Do you understand what I'm telling you?"

I shrugged. "I guess."

"Please, Luke. This is real stuff. We're not in Saratoga right now. Neither are the Shaheens."

"I get it, okay?"

He studied me. Sighed. Then he opened his bag, and heaved up a pile of folders and papers.

"Well, I've got a bunch of work to do. We had a good first day, Assad and I—tomorrow we'll go out to some of the ruins. Do some photography. Think you might like to come?" He asked this casually, but he was watching.

"I'm…kind of liking hanging around here. For now."

"Well…want to hang with me a little while? You could listen to your music."

"Maybe in a minute," I said. "I think I'll go out front and look at the traffic. It's kind of weirdly entertaining."

"Okay. But stay right out front."

And he started back in, with his papers and his work. Like always.

I leaned against the railing, watching the evening traffic clatter through the intersection. I was starting to see how these truck and taxi drivers, riders of scooters and bicycles, peddlers of bicycle rickshaws, pullers of carts, and pedestrians in pajamas and flapping sandals were all doing what they had to do. Making it through.

"You have this in the U.S.? This traffic?"

Surprised, I turned to see Yusuf.

"Uh, well, we have traffic, but not like this. We have lanes and stoplights. It's…different."

He smiled. "At first it looks like madness—but everyone must go someplace. People make way."

"I was kind of seeing that, actually."

"Yes." He reached into a front pocket of his jeans. "I brought some things. To show."

"Oh yeah? Like what?"

He brought out a cassette, home-recorded and hand-labeled in its case. He put it in my hand, and I held it up to catch the light. Careful penmanship on the card behind the clear cover said *Catch a Fire* and *Burnin'*.

"Bob and the Wailers' first albums on Island Records!" I said. "These are classics, man."

"This is true?"

"Oh yeah."

Now he was taking out a folded paper, which he opened almost lovingly and placed in my hand. It was a page from a magazine: a glossy photo of Bob Marley on stage, his denim shirt open, eyes closed like he was singing in a trance. Long dreadlocks whirled around his head.

"Cool. Where'd you get these things?"

"The music, in Kabul. On Chicken Street."

"*Chicken* Street?" I laughed.

"Yes, you can get anything there. I heard Bobmarli in a cafe, and I wanted this. Then, in this hotel after we came here, someone left a Western magazine. When I looked inside, I saw this photo."

Yusuf looked at his treasures in my hands. "These are special to me," he said.

"Is this all you have? Of Bob?"

"Yes."

"Oh, man! I've got a lot more you can hear. I can go get it right now."

"No, no. There is time."

Yusuf was looking out at the intersection. I felt there was more, like something he wanted to say. We watched the traffic dodge and swirl.

"I always remember when I heard the first song," Yusuf said. "On the first side?"

"'Concrete Jungle'—oh yeah," I said. "Right away you know this is *something*."

He nodded. "When I hear that, I know that he knows. I don't think he came to Kabul, or Peshawar..."

"I don't think so, man."

"But it's the same," Yusuf said, watching the traffic. "So much struggle. People have dreams. He knows."

"When he was our age he lived in Trenchtown," I said. "That's a really poor neighborhood in Kingston. The capital of Jamaica."

Yusuf nodded. I wanted to run up and get my tapes. But something made me stay, and wait. Finally Yusuf spoke again.

"I would like to take you. On a short walk only. With permission of course."

"Where?"

He held a hand out toward the corner on the left, and the street that led back from it. "Just up there is a way into the Old City. I have friends there. I think it will be interesting for you—and they will like to meet you. They are good guys."

"Well..." I thought about it. "I have to ask my dad. If I just went he'd freak."

"Of course."

Nested among his papers in the dining room, my dad peered up in surprise.

"The Old City?"

"Yeah. He says it's a short walk."

"It is very near," Yusuf said, coming up behind. "Hello, Professor." He shook my dad's hand.

"You'd need to be very careful," my dad said to him. "Luke's never been in a place like this."

"Of course. Do not worry, please. I am a Pashtun man."

"Well...okay. But be back in an hour or so, boys, all right? Or else I'll worry."

"You don't have to worry, sir," Yusuf said.

My dad nodded. "I understand. You're a Pashtun man."

In the night the street led, wide at first, back from the hotel toward a murky dimness that was crowded with low, squeezed-together buildings. We walked by a still-open shop, a narrow lighted space with stacks of cigarettes, sweets and soda. The shopkeeper sat on a platform in the opening, surrounded by his goods, as skinny men walked by wrapped in blankets.

The street rose, grew darker, and cramped into a narrow right turn. Here the shops were shut, and the lane was maybe a dozen feet wide. Dark buildings sagged over our heads, shuttered tight and really, really old. I felt like I had stepped back five hundred years.

Yusuf strode on and I trailed him, looking around at this dark passage, and suddenly we were in a meat district. In tiny shops like open caves, oil lanterns cast yellow glows on hanging reddish carcasses and men who worked the meat on slick wood floors. Their cleavers glinted, rising and falling: *thunk thunk thunk.*

Here on the uneven lane, a cart piled with carcasses was being pushed and pulled along by thin men who jumped around it, shoving and straining to keep it from tipping over. The wood wheels creaked, the cart tilted, and a skinned limb flopped out from the cargo.

We kept moving and came to a quiet section. The shuttered dark buildings crowded together like they were leaning over us, watching. Then up ahead I saw light, and a busy little corner. We walked faster as we came up to it.

A cigarette-and-soda shop was brightly open at this tiny intersection. Outside it, a small crowd of boys and men stood around a cart that was piled with peanuts. Then the boys and men spotted us, and we were surrounded.

In front were young men in short-sleeved shirts with open collars. Behind them were skinny, bug-eyed guys, wrapped in blankets and bouncing on tiptoes to get a better look...at me. All their brown eyes fastened on me, and stayed fastened as they bobbed up and down. I didn't like this, it was weird. I wanted to go home, turn around, get away. I knew the way, it was straight back there; I was about to turn and go when a guy in a patterned shirt, not much older than Yusuf and me, reached into the pile on the cart and took out a peanut.

"In our language it's easy," he said. "*Mung pahli.*"

He held up the peanut, and smiled. I was a little embarrassed.

"Mung pahli," I said, to the peanut.

"Yes!" Everyone smiled, nodded.

"Please do not mind these people," the guy said. He had an open, friendly face. Behind him, the skinny ones in blankets kept bobbing up and down. "These are simple people," the guy said. "They only want to see you."

"I guess."

"May I ask, what is your country?"

"America."

"*Am*'rica!" There was a flurry of discussion, sounding like approval.

"Please don't mind," the young man said again. "These guys don't know how to speak to you."

"But your English is good."

"I am studying at the PACC—the Pakistan-American Cultural Center," he said. "I have completed third-level English. I like to study languages." He stuck out his hand. "I am Imtiaz."

We shook. "Luke," I said.

"Luck?"

"Luke."

"Ah—yes. It's good to look."

"No, I mean that's my name."

"Yes! A joke."

"It's not a joke, it's my—"

"Yes, no, sorry! I was trying to make a joke, but it was *bad*." The guys beside him laughed. *These must be Yusuf's friends,* I thought.

One was bright-eyed and quick-smiling, with a thin mustache like an old-time movie star. The other had a round face and stayed quiet.

Our group went over to a closed-up shop whose front was covered by a metal grate, pulled down and secured with a big brass padlock. Here it was darker. We sat on the ledge. No one else around, now.

Imtiaz said, "Are you a student?"

"Yeah, high school. Ninth grade."

"Is it good? The school?"

I shrugged. "It's high school." The guys nodded, listening.

"After this," Imtiaz said, "you can go to college?"

"Yeah. My dad teaches at a college, actually. So I can go for cheaper."

Then I felt kind of bad. "Can you...I mean, there's college here, right?"

"Yes, for some," Imtiaz said. "I have a master's degree."

"You do? What in?"

"Political science. And I speak four languages."

"Whoa! That's amazing."

He shrugged. "It doesn't matter. There are no jobs."

I looked at the other guys, sitting on the ledge. The bright-eyed one shrugged.

"There must be *some* jobs," I said.

"Only for those with *approach*," Imtiaz said. "You have to know someone powerful, or you must have money. If you don't have these things, you have no chance."

"Huh."

"We have friends who left," Imtiaz said, brightening. "They went to Iran, France. We have their photos, we can show you."

I had no clue what to say. I liked these guys, though. The shops around us were all padlocked; the upper stories loomed in darkness, antique wood shutters tightly closed over the windows. I wondered: were the girls up there? In there? Somewhere?

"I have a photo," Imtiaz said.

"Oh yeah? What of?"

He reached in his pocket, brought it out. "This is my class at the PACC. On commencement day." The picture showed two ranks of serious young men and one serious American woman, their teacher. In the picture, Imtiaz's head was shaved.

"You shaved your head!"

"Yes. I cut it all."

"But why?"

"Because I have given up on my country." He shouted suddenly, into the darkness: "We want no narrow-minded people here! *Only broad-minded people here!*"

I looked up and down the murky streets. I wondered if it was dangerous, in a place like this, to yell stuff like that.

"This is my shop," said the bright-eyed guy. He nodded at the grate behind us. "Radio repair. Also TV. Tomorrow, please come. For a visit."

I looked at Yusuf. He nodded.

"I would like that," I said.

"Yes—please. You must come."

Imtiaz stood up. "Let's take tea," he said, and he led our group back up the lane.

In the wide part back near the hotel, us five stooped into a little teashop. In dingy yellow light we sat on wood benches at a scarred table. Our tea came sweet and brown, in clear plastic glasses. I sipped mine, wondering how I could be here.

"Tell me how I can go to America," said Imtiaz.

"Huh? You want to?"

"I must go. America is the best place. How can I go?"

"I don't know. Really."

"Please. Please tell me. I must go."

"I don't know," I said again. "I don't know anything about that stuff. I'm sorry."

"Please," he said. His face and eyes were pleading. I had no idea what to tell him. It was awkward.

Yusuf stood up. "We have promised your father," he said. "We must go."

I finished my tea and stood, and we shook the young men's hands. The others said good night politely, but Imtiaz did not. He kept on sitting and staring, his face flushed, at the nicked-up table and the yellowed walls.

As Yusuf and I walked back, I said, "Those are your friends, right?"

"Yes. My friends."

"Seem like decent guys."

"Oh yes, good guys. But you see, there is frustration."

"Yeah."

"People feel they cannot make a good life here."

"Huh."

Close to the hotel, the shops were closed now. A man lay wrapped in a blanket on the ground, sleeping between the wheels of his cart. Yusuf stopped walking. I did, too. He seemed...preoccupied.

"Something on your mind?" I asked.

Yusuf looked into my eyes, then at the ground. "Maybe," he said. "Maybe there is something."

"Tell me."

"I do not want to be impolite."

"Don't worry. I'm impolite all the time."

He looked puzzled.

"I mean, go ahead," I said. "What is it?"

He was silent for another moment. Then: "That man today. At the cafe, in the new town."

"I meant to ask you about that," I said. "How come you didn't come in?"

He sort of shrugged, but didn't answer. He asked, "What do you know about that guy?"

"Not much. He said he's from Saudi Arabia. He's friends with Rashi. They're in that group, with that guesthouse. Hey," I said, as I remembered something from last night, "is that the group that wants to be holy warriors?"

Yusuf was staring at the ground. Now he looked up.

"These people are *Wahhabis*," he said. *Wah-HAH-bees*, he pronounced it.

"They're what?"

"Wahhabis. I wasn't sure until your friend mentioned the Services Bureau. Everyone knows who has this house. The Wahhabi way comes from Saudi Arabia."

"O...kay..."

"These are extreme people."

"What do you mean?"

"This is *not* true Islam," he burst out. "They say they come to help the mujahideen, but they don't *khyr* about Afghan people."

"They don't what?"

"They don't care about people—they only care what they believe. They think their belief should rule the world."

"That guy seemed okay. Basically."

"I'm saying to you, *be careful*. In my country I have seen what people like this can do."

He turned away, and walked fast into the hotel. I watched him go, then shrugged and came along behind.

In the lobby, a desk clerk said, "Sir? Hello?"

"Hi."

"There is a message for you."

"For me?"

He handed me an envelope. On it was written, in neat and careful handwriting:

> *For Mr. Luke Sands*
> *Personal and Confidential*

I stuck the envelope in my pocket, took my room key and went upstairs. I heard *pock pock pock **ping!*** next door. I closed my door and ripped open the envelope.

Inside was a single, folded sheet of cream-colored paper.

> *Please come for tea tomorrow. Please come late in the afternoon, between 4 and 5 p.m. We are preparing tea for you. Please come.*

There was no signature, no return address, but I recognized the careful handwriting from the postcard she had sent asking for *Thriller.*

I read the note two or three more times. Then I put on my headphones and slipped *Catch a Fire* into the Walkman. As I stood looking out my window at the cobbled lane below, "Concrete Jungle" rose up strong from the silence and I thought about a lot of things.

How must it feel to be Dani—to have lived in the U.S. for a whole year, going to school with American kids, then to come back here? Did she have to wear that blue thing, or would she? What were "extreme people"? Why did Rashi have a fake name, and why didn't Dani sign her name? And if I was Dani's friend...how dangerous could that be?

I put the invitation in the bottom of my backpack, where no one would find it.

5.
Our Honor

I HAD A HARD TIME getting to sleep. Then that typing woke me up again, way too early in the morning. I lay there getting madder and madder. At him.

He never wanted this coming here to be some father-son thing. It was always about him—him and his stupid work. I really did hate it. I hated the typing, hated the project, hated his obsession and what it had done to my family. I wanted a different dad for Christmas.

Christmas. I was completely missing it. How was that even possible? I lay there looking at the bare blue walls, the same color as those weird things the women had to wear. Why did he *bring* me here? Him and his stupid goddamn project.

*Pock pock whack pock **ping**!*

I told him I didn't want to come down for breakfast. Through the closed door, he asked if I was going to stay inside this morning. I grunted.

"Luke, I need an answer."

"I don't know."

"That's not an answer."

"Whatever."

"What?"

"I'm…not…going…out this morning," I said, loudly. "All right?" I didn't say anything about the afternoon.

Long pause. "Okay. Luke, I don't want you going anywhere without me knowing about it—and not without Yusuf. Not *anywhere*, even just outside the hotel. Do you read me?"

Do you read me. What a dork.

"Luke?"

"*Okay.*"

Longer pause. Then: "Is he all right? Yusuf? Do you like him?"

"He's okay."

"Do you trust him?"

I thought about that. "I do, actually. He's a decent guy."

"Well...good. Assad says the same thing. Sure you don't want to come down? Aren't you hungry?"

"No," I said, which wasn't true. I was too tired to think straight and too angry to go back to sleep, but I was *really* hungry. I just didn't want to deal with him.

"O...kay," he said, and went away.

I listened to music for a while, pulling the 'phones away from my ears now and then until, finally, I heard the typing start up again. Then I got up and went downstairs.

I had porridge, which is what they called oatmeal here. If you spooned enough sugar on it, it wasn't bad. I was drinking qawa, sugar in that too, when Rasheed came hurrying in through the front doors and the lobby, into the dining room. He was wearing long-tailed pajamas today, like most everyone else here. He strode fast to my table and sat.

"Hey, bro," he said. "How are you?"

"Okay."

"You're done, right?"

"Huh?"

"You're done eating." He glanced at my oatmeal. I wasn't done.

"Why?"

"I'm right out front," he said, very quietly. "Wait a couple of minutes, then come out. Okay?"

"Uh...I guess."

My dad had said no going outside alone, not even out front. Therefore, that was what I would do.

He stood up. "Great," he said more loudly. "See you!"

I spooned up the rest of the porridge. Yusuf came to clear the table; I stood up without saying anything, and walked through the little plain lobby to the street.

The intersection was roiled with intense morning traffic. Out here it was totally noisy, horns blaring everywhere; fumes clogged the air, and suddenly I was doubled over, coughing. I felt dizzy. When finally I could breathe again, I saw that Rashi was standing at the railing with Amal, who smiled.

"My friend! Hello," Amal said, and we shook hands. Today he had on a gray nylon track suit, three white stripes down the arms and legs, and Adidas Superstars. The shoes looked new. Bright white leather.

"You are well?" he asked. Beside him Rashi nodded eagerly.

"I think I'm okay," I said.

"God be thanked. It's good to see you."

"Yeah, um…you too."

Professor Shaheen had told me people might want to talk with me and so forth, and that I should trust my instincts—I did remember that. But the thing about Amal was, I didn't have a bad impression of him. It was more…like he knew what he was doing. That he was smooth, and he wasn't telling me everything. I didn't know what that meant, but it was the feeling I had.

I looked at the traffic. All the fumes and noise were hard to take. Hadn't slept enough.

"I want you to know we have kept the promise we made," Amal said. He glanced at Rashi, who nodded.

"We have not spoken about our conversation, about your family business, to anyone else," Amal said. "You remember we made this promise, yes? Perhaps you have not spoken of it either."

"Um, nope." That was true, I hadn't told Yusuf what we talked about. He just said I should be careful.

"Then good—we have each kept faith." Amal leaned in closer, through the clamor and fumes. "Here is another question. This trouble that has so burdened your family—what if it could go away?"

"Huh?"

"If this problem could simply, quickly"—he snapped his fingers—"be gone, and you and your family would be free of it. If this could happen in an easy, peaceful manner, it would be a good thing, yes?"

"Yeah, it would."

"And if you could help this to happen, would you?"

"Well, if I could. Sure."

"Actually, in a small way, you *can* help," he said. "So I think you are saying yes."

"I guess so, sure. But what do you mean?"

"I will leave it to our brother to tell you more. And now you are one of us—truly," Amal said, and he held out his hand. We shook hands. That's what people here did.

"We are a brotherhood," he said, "and on our honor we keep our promises. And now I must go. It's a busy day! *Inshallah,* all will be well."

He shook my hand again, turned and was gone around the corner.

I turned back to Rasheed. "What was *that* about?"

"*Inshallah?*" He smiled. "It means 'if God wills it, it will happen.' Only then."

"Okay. What about the rest of it?"

"Today is Wednesday," he said as a truck roared by.

"What?"

"It is Wednesday! In two days it will be Friday—our day of prayer."

I pinched my nose. My head hurt. "Rashi ..."

"Every Friday, all over the world, Muslims go to the mosque at midday and pray. Actually, every day we offer prayers, but on Friday we make them all together. It's fantastic! You will see!" He was nodding and smiling.

"Rashi, start making sense. Okay?"

"After prayers on Friday, my family has invited you and your father to luncheon, at Dean's Hotel. It's a special place, really nice. Expensive! But you will be our guests."

"All right…"

He leaned in close. "When you leave to take this special meal, the key will be in the door between your room and your father's."

"What? How did you know…"

"It doesn't matter. When you leave, just leave that key there, and forget to lock your door. The one from the hallway into your room, forget to lock it. That's all."

"What?"

"It's nothing! You're not used to staying in a hotel, so you forget to do this. Or not do it. You won't actually *do* anything." He smiled.

I stepped back. "Rashi, what are you talking about?"

"It will be simple, and no one will be hurt," he said. "That's all you need to know."

"No it isn't. What are you *talking* about?"

"Luke. Did you know that idol worship is the first sin? In both our faiths?"

"Is this you explaining?"

"Yes! The first of your Ten Commandments says, *Thou shalt have no other gods before me*. And we say, *There is no God but God*. This is how we begin our declaration of faith, that we make every day. Every day!"

"Okay, so…"

"So if someone glorifies objects that are not God, because objects cannot *be* God, this is idol worship. And idolatry is the first sin—the *worst* sin. What we're doing is *right*."

"You are possibly the world's worst explainer, Rashi."

"No! We are freeing these men, Luke—freeing our families, freeing this place. Of the *first sin*."

"What men?" Then it hit me. "Wait—you mean our *dads*?"

He nodded, just slightly.

"Our dads," I said. "Yours and mine. You want me to leave my door unlocked, so you can…"

"So the sin will be gone. Then we will be free—and you can go home. For Christmas!"

I stared at him. This was too bizarre.

"You have shaken hands on this—made a promise on your honor," he said. "You have to keep it."

"Don't tell me what I have to do, just tell me what this is about. Exactly."

"Luke, you don't—"

"*Exactly*, Rashi. Or I go to our dads and tell them something's up."

He shook his head. "Luke. Do you understand what this book of theirs is about?"

"Um…maybe not exactly."

"Well, I do. They want to glorify a civilization that was in this valley a lot of centuries ago—one that was all about worshipping stone idols. This is wrong, Luke. To promote idolatry is *wrong*."

"But…they're just historians, man. Who cares? Why make some big deal about it?"

He was silent for a moment. Then he said, "There's a *fatwa*."

"A what?"

"A fatwa. It's an edict, an order from an elder of the faith. A fatwa must be carried out."

"By who?"

"By us! The brotherhood. You and me and…"

"What does this thing say?"

Rashi glanced around, like he wanted to be sure no one was listening.

"It says the idolatry must be consumed."

"Consumed? How?"

"In the fire of faith."

"Rasheed, what are you *talking* about?"

"A fatwa must be followed."

"Or else what?"

"There is no *or else*. A fatwa must be followed."

I stepped back, trying to think. It was so noisy, so fumy.

"So…you want me to leave my door unlocked, so you can—"

"Not me."

"So *somebody* can…what, burn the room? Burn the hotel?"

"No! No one will be injured," he said. "But we cannot allow the base for our new movement of faith to become famous for the *worst* crime against God. It's our duty to remove the sin."

Finally it hit me. "Your friends want to steal our dads' *work*? Their *book*?"

"Not steal. Commit to the fire."

"So they *do* want to burn the hotel."

"No! Only this work. It is idolatry—it must be committed to the fire."

"And you're okay with this."

"It is God's will."

"How do *you* know that?"

"Because our holy book tells me." He began to recite: *"And say to those to whom the Book has been given, 'Do you surrender to God?' And if they have surrendered, they are rightly guided. But if they turn away, your only responsibility is to deliver a message."*

I just stared at him.

"Our holy book is a complete program for living—it tells us everything," Rashi said. "The father of my flesh has gone astray. It's our duty to bring him back."

"But isn't your dad Muslim?"

"He says so, but has gone astray. *If they turn away, your only responsibility is to deliver a message.*"

"How can you be so sure?"

"If they have surrendered, they are rightly guided. Our faith is all about surrendering to God's will." He smiled. "We believe and we are rightly guided."

"We're talking about a crime here, Rashi."

"To act against idolatry is no crime in God's eyes."

"What if your guys get caught? Have you *thought* about this?"

"Luke…look. If the brothers can get the work, they will burn it up. And that will be the end of it." He nodded, hard. "But if they can't get it…"

"Then what? What happens then?"

He shrugged. "A fatwa must be carried out. It's a duty."

"Rashi…don't you think this is a little nuts?"

He shook his head. "Luke, the world today is sick—it's a mess, okay? People are obsessed with money, with drugs and sex and things to buy, and we brothers have the only cure. And if we *have* the cure, should we not bring it to the world? Doesn't everyone who has a sickness really want, in their hearts, to be cured?"

"Who put out this thing?"

"What thing?"

"This fatwa."

"It doesn't matter."

"Yes it does. Who?"

"An elder, like I told you. He's a wise and generous man."

"What's his name?"

"Sheikh Osama, but that's not important. Only God is important. Look around you, Luke—open your heart to the truth. Then you will see."

"Rashi, I don't think…"

"But you're *learning,*" he said quickly, and smiled. "Have a great day, Luke. Keep faith. Tomorrow we'll speak again."

He held out his hand. I didn't shake it. He turned away and walked around the corner. I stood there, staring at the traffic, for a long time.

6.

Mister Look

LATER, WHEN I'D FINISHED my rice pudding from lunch, I was sitting at the table staring at the wall. I could go to Dani's house in three hours. I wished that was all I had to think about.

Yusuf came up. He'd taken off his white jacket.

"Lunch was good?" he said.

"Um…yeah…"

He nodded, but didn't sit. "This morning, I have spoken with your father," he said.

"Huh? About what?"

"I would like us to visit the Old City again. He has given permission."

"Well, okay…but we went last night."

"Yes—and we promised to visit our friend with the radio shop. Remember?"

"Oh. Right."

"Also," he said, "there is someone else I want you to meet."

"Yeah? Another of your guys?"

"Not exactly. You will see."

I figured, why not? Maybe this would take my mind off things.

"Let's go," I said.

Above the meat shops, the ancient upper stories loomed and sagged. They were shuttered tight, even in daylight, but last night's little crossroads was lively and busy now. The bright-eyed guy sat at the open front of his shop, behind a glass cabinet a step above the lane. He stood and spread wide his arms.

"Hello, my friends! Welcome!"

His name, he said, was Nasim. He wore a brown blazer over blue pajamas, and behind him rose a tall metal shelf crammed with battered-looking radios and televisions. At a workbench in back, a teenage boy bent with a soldering iron over the guts of a TV.

Nasim called out, and at a teashop across the lane, a boy put white cups and two pots on a tray and hurried this way, through the mingling passing men. The boy set the tray on Nasim's glass counter, then darted back.

"You like green tea?" Nasim asked, waving at the two pots. "Black?"

"Qawa," I said.

"Oh, you know!" He poured from one of the pots, and motioned toward two chairs. "Please, sit. Relax. We will take tea."

We drank, and when our cups were empty Nasim poured more. Across the lane, I saw how the little teashop was the busy center of this neighborhood. On a tiny platform above the street sat the jowly tea-maker beside two big copper urns. From a little silver faucet at the base of each one, he'd draw the steaming tea—one spigot gave out black tea, I could see, the other one green—into little teapots. Then he'd crush seeds and sprinkle them into the pots of green, swirling tea and seeds together to make the qawa.

When each pot was ready, the man would set it on the ledge—and it would be picked up quickly by one of the boys who kept moving, taking cups and trays of tea, threading through the traffic, bringing back empties and starting off again. It was like a dance. I wondered how long it had been going on.

"How old is this place?"

"My shop?" Nasim said. "A few years only."

"No, I mean this neighborhood."

"It is called Karim Pura Bazaar."

"Okay. So how old is it? I mean, do you know?"

"Maybe two thousand years." Nasim shrugged. "Who can know?"

"Two *thousand* years?"

"Maybe more." He grinned. "Who can know?"

Outside the shop, men walked the lane in loose white turbans and woolen caps with rolled edges, in pale pajamas and wrapped-around blankets, in sandals and flip-flops. It was like seeing into some age long ago, except for the flip-flops. Then a motor scooter blatted through, its young rider cocky in a silver racing jacket as he rumbled past bicyclists on the rumple-surfaced lane. A man swatted the neck of an ox as it slowly, slowly pulled a cart piled high with thick-filled sacks.

"So, like, is everyone here Muslim?"

"Of course, in Peshawar," Nasim said. "Except for some guests," he said, and bowed to me.

"There is a Christian church," Yusuf said to him. "Inside Kohati Gate." They said something in Pashto. Nasim nodded.

"You can find anything here," he said. "If you wait and watch, you will *see* anything."

We sat and watched a while. Then Yusuf said, "Luke has met some Wahhabis."

Nasim's head drew back. "Have you?"

"Um...I guess so. They're, like, friends of this guy I know."

"Are they...your friends as well?" He was cooler now.

"I don't think so," I said.

"They are not Pakistani."

"No. Well, my friend is."

"Oh? Is he Pashtun?"

"Yeah. I know his family. So what do you think? I mean really."

Nasim and Yusuf talked in Pashto for a moment. Then Nasim said, "They are strong believers, these guys. We are too, in Peshawar. But we don't feel so good about them coming here."

"No? Why not?"

"Well…when these people first came, maybe a year ago, they said they come to support the mujahideen. Okay, good. Then they say they will fight *with* the mujahideen. Okay, fine. They start bringing young guys from other countries, to be jihadis. Fine, fine—but now they are telling us that everyone here must be perfect Muslims. We must be pure. And *they* are saying what this means."

"How?"

"How?"

"Yeah. How do they say that?"

"Oh, their Sheikh Azzam is often speaking in the mosques. They put out cassettes of his talks—those are all over the city. Also they publish a magazine. Even though they are new in Peshawar, these people are giving a very loud message."

"What's the message?"

"They say if you don't think the right way, God doesn't like you," Nasim said. "Maybe God hates you."

"Even if you're Muslim?"

Nasim shrugged. "We're all Muslim here. And we're intelligent people—we read things, we know about the world. We don't need someone to tell us what to think."

Yusuf spoke up: "In my country, this happened."

"In Afghanistan?"

He nodded. "For a long time we had peace. Work hard, believe in God, take care of the family, you know? Then we got extreme people on both sides."

He was saying this to me. Like he wanted me to get it.

"In Kabul were the Reds and the Greens—Communists and Islamists," Yusuf said. "Reds and Greens don't like each other, so they fight. First it was just words, and the schools and colleges got divided. The Communists tell you how to think, what to say and do. They hate the Islamists. The Islamists, *they* tell you what to think, how to believe—and they hate the Communists.

"The Reds get power, so the Greens fight. The Reds are about to fall, so the big Communists, the Soviet Russians—they come in, with machine guns and tanks.

"The Reds throw thousands of men in prison. They kill many more, and the Islamists fight back. *They* kill people. If one side thinks you're on the other side, they kill you.

"Both sides say they are always right," Yusuf said. "Both sides. And by this my country is being destroyed."

"But you said the Wahhabis come from Saudi Arabia."

"Yes. They rule that country, with the king and his family."

"We have Islamists in Pakistan also—but these men are foreigners," Nasim said. "They are too much extreme."

"So you don't like those guys."

"It is not a matter of not liking," Nasim said. "We are *afraid* of these guys." He thought for a second. Then he waved at the metal rack behind him.

"Sometimes I think we are all like these radios—every one is a little bit broken. No one can be perfect like the Holy Prophet, peace be upon him. If you don't agree with the Wahhabis, they say God hates you. How can *they* know?"

"I don't know," I said.

"Well, neither do I." He turned to sell a bit of wire to a man at the counter. When he turned back, he said, "I am a shopkeeper, what do I know? But I say, be careful of these men."

"That's what Yusuf said."

"He has seen too much," Nasim said softly, looking at Yusuf.

My Afghan friend stood up. "Now we go," he said.

"Stay! Take more tea," Nasim said. "I want to hear stories of America."

"I'll come back," I said, because I wanted to. I liked this guy.

"Where do you go now?"

"Qissa Khwani Bazaar," Yusuf said.

"Ah—the Storytellers' Bazaar!" Nasim grinned his big smile.

"The what?"

"The Street of Storytellers," he said. "In old times in Peshawar, you could buy anything in the world. Over the mountain passes came silver, spices, silks, gems to trade, really everything—from China, Persia, Europe, by caravans of men and horses and camels. Yaks for the high mountains.

"With the caravans came many stories," he went on. "So this place, our biggest bazaar—it had storytellers. Maybe you would pay one rupee to hear a tale of Iskandar. Or Issa."

"And they were..."

"Iskandar was Alexander the Great, the famous conqueror from Europe," Nasim said. "Issa was your Jesus Christ."

"Whoa. Really?"

"Sure—a great prophet. We honor him. So, you will see! Qissa Khwani Bazaar is the heart of old Peshawar."

We all shook hands. As Yusuf and I started up the lane, Nasim called out, "Good luck, Mister Look!"

7.

A Seller of Cloth

DEEPER INTO THE OLD CITY, I followed Yusuf along a street that grew busier and wider as we went along, and more like a dream. It was filled with crowds of men in loose turbans and rolled caps who moved in every direction, all ways at once, everyone strangely calm. Their dusty tide opened for a darting bicycle, then closed to swallow motorcycles, scooter rickshaws, bicycle rickshaws.

Along the edge, Yusuf led us past carts of orange and banana sellers, past wide pans where men simmered meat in popping oil, by rickety stalls where peddlers had made high piles of random-seeming things—shoe polish, sunglasses, baby formula, plastic flowers. A man had a pole slung across his shoulders, and from each end hung a wire cage filled with parrots. They were bright green, and seemed sad.

I stumbled along. Anything could pop up. I smelled bananas. Two boys in turbans stood talking face to face: one had a basket of flowers balanced on his turban, the other a basket of bloody goat hooves. This was the strangest of dreams.

We passed crippled people begging in the dirt, and an old woman with hair in matted cords like dreadlocks, shaking, hand out for coins. The street was scattered with orange peels. Bent-over old people went by leaning on staffs; well-dressed men sat upright on rickshaws pulled by skinny guys straining on bicycles. Boys threaded past with trays of tea.

Yusuf pushed ahead steadily through everything. I struggled to follow. "Where are we?"

"This is Old Peshawar! You like it?"

"It's kind of wild!"

"Yes."

"Are we really going to see someone?"

"Yes."

"Who?"

"You will see!"

He kept plunging forward. I was behind him in the swallowing crowd, doing my best to keep his dark, bobbing head in sight.

Shopkeepers leaned out to catch my eye. I shook hands with one; another offered an orange, which I stuck in my pocket. A little man, squatting by a blackened pan with fish frying in it, called out as I passed, "What is your country?"

I turned back. "America!"

"Ah!" The man grinned and pointed upward. "First god is God," he said. "Second god is America!"

Down a narrow alley, old men and little kids sat on benches under tin awnings. In a shaft of light at the alley's end was a tiny white mosque, with a dome like an eggshell. A woman hurried by, shrouded and shapeless in a burqa, then turned down the alley and disappeared.

Yusuf turned into a narrow lane of cloth sellers that had long, colored banners hanging from its upper stories. This lane looked so medieval that I half expected to see knights in armor striding by—but women in burqas squatted inside the narrow shops. They chattered as merchants unrolled bolts of beautiful colors and shimmering patterns. I didn't understand. Where did they *wear* cloth like that? What did they do with it?

Yusuf stooped into a shop. Its floor was covered in deeply patterned carpet, and stacked high were bolts of bright cloth: yellows, reds, golds and silvers, turquoise and paisley. Yusuf shook hands with the shopkeeper, who sat cross-legged on a cushion by the entrance. Yusuf turned to introduce him.

"This is Pir Sahib," he said. "I have told him about you."

The man had a neat white chin beard, and his spreading smile was the warmest I had ever seen, or felt. His white-and-gold-patterned turban was perfectly wound; one end hung down neatly by his brown wool vest and pure-white pajamas. His eyes shone, and he just seemed...I don't know...kind. As he looked in my eyes, a bright warmness spread inside me. Like everything was okay.

When Pir Sahib looked down, the warmness faded, and he was nodding at me to sit. I sat down shakily on a cushion, by Yusuf on the carpet. A boy appeared as if by magic, with a tray of tea and sugar biscuits. Pir Sahib poured qawa for us, and spread his hand toward the biscuits. I took one and ate half. It tasted simple and sweet, like childhood.

The man spoke to Yusuf in Pashto.

"Pir Sahib says he watched you coming along this lane," Yusuf said. "He could see you were thinking about something. Maybe a question. He asks, what is it?"

"Well..."

"It's okay," Yusuf said. "Anything, you can ask."

"Well, this cloth. All these colors," I said. "Do women wear them?"

"Yes. Sure."

"But, like where? I don't see where."

Yusuf translated the question. Answering, smiling, the shopkeeper tapped his chest.

"He says inside. Indoors. Where the heart is."

Yusuf smiled too—his face lit up, and I saw how handsome he was. I hadn't seen him smile before.

The shopkeeper leaned forward. He said, "And for you?"

"Huh?"

Gently, he asked, "What is in your heart?"

I didn't know he spoke English. I heard myself say, "I don't...It's just...I don't want to hurt my dad." I was really surprised that I said that.

He nodded. "We don't like to hurt our fathers," he said. "They are working hard."

I looked down. "Yeah."

"But why is *this* in your heart?"

"Well, I mean...some people want me to help them do something," I said. "They want to take away this work he's been doing—a book he's writing. They say it's..." I swallowed. "They say it's idol worship."

I was afraid he'd get angry. But he didn't.

"Some men say this?"

"Yeah. I mean yes. And I was really mad at my dad, 'cause he worked so much on this book that my mom got a divorce. But these guys want to burn the whole thing—they say if I help them, we can go home and it'll all be fixed. But I just...I don't get it. Why is everyone so worked up about a book? Why does my *dad* care so much?"

Yusuf was just listening. The shopkeeper said, "You are far from home."

"Oh yeah."

"Your father has brought you here."

"Yes."

"Because of this work?"

I nodded.

"Hmm." Now he was looking down. At my sneakers.

"Oh," I said, "I'm sorry—I can take these off." I started to, but he held up his hand. He was still peering at them.

"But...these are not your father's shoes," he said, like he was surprised.

I couldn't help it; I snorted. "No!"

He looked up, a sparkle in his eyes. "Then you must trade!"

"What? Why?"

"Why not?" He grinned, like this was the best joke. "How can you know someone's heart if you have not gone where he goes, and walked in his shoes?"

We sat there. I went, "Huh."

Pir Sahib motioned again at the biscuits. "Please."

I took one, and ate it. He watched me, and for a while we didn't say anything. Then he nodded.

"We have many sayings of our Prophet Muhammad," the shopkeeper said. "One is, 'Go in search of knowledge—even if you must go to China.'"

"Huh."

"But this is not China. Only Peshawar!" He actually giggled. I nodded, like *That's* true. Then he said, "So where? Where can you go to look?"

When I didn't answer, Pir Sahib took my hands in his. "There is a place," he said. "Go to that place."

I said, "Um…"

He let go my hands, and sipped his tea again. Over the cup his eyes sparkled, like now we shared a secret. Maybe we did; I just didn't know what it was.

Pir Sahib turned to Yusuf. "Perhaps you will visit the *dargah*," he said. "Together."

Yusuf nodded. And he stood up.

"Now we go," he said to me.

We came out from the medieval lane onto a gassy, hot, crowded street where spangled trucks, painted rickshaws and turbaned men flowed thickly everywhere. I dodged along. Then I yelled, "Who is that guy?"

"He is Pir Sahib!" Yusuf, ahead, called over his shoulder.

"Yeah, but who *is* he?"

"He is a seller of cloth!"

I caught up and grabbed Yusuf's sleeve. I hadn't done that here, hadn't touched someone. I didn't know what would happen.

Yusuf stopped, turned back.

"He isn't just a seller of cloth," I said. "Is he?" I let go. "Sorry."

He shrugged. "He is a kind of teacher," Yusuf said. "I am not an actual student of his—to be that, you must make a big commitment, to study and work very hard. But I go to take tea with him. When I was new to Peshawar, he talked with me. He helped me. It is an honor that he has invited you to the dargah."

"What is that?"

"It's a shrine, a place that honors one of our saints. Pir Sahib teaches there."

"So…is he like a holy man?"

Yusuf shrugged again. "*Pir* means teacher, like a wise man. You can say holy man if you like."

"But he has a shop!"

"Yes. Why not?"

"Is he a Wahhabi?"

Yusuf's eyes widened; he laughed. "What do *you* think?"

"I don't think so, but…Rashi said the Wahhabis have a wise man."

Yusuf looked down for a second, then up at me. "Wahhabis tell you what to think," he said. "If you don't agree, they say you are not a true Muslim. Pir Sahib asks you questions—he helps you *see*. That is a big difference, I think."

"Yeah. Oh yeah."

I peered at Yusuf, because now maybe I did see something.

"You brought me out today so we could talk with those guys. Right? First Nasim. Then Pir Sahib."

"We promised Nasim we would visit his shop."

"Yeah, but there was more. I mean there was. Right?"

Again, he shrugged.

"Okay," I said, "here's what I think. You wanted me to talk with those guys because you know what Rasheed and his friends are trying to get me to do. You wanted me to see the other side, or whatever."

From the look on his face, I knew I had it. "That's it, right?"

"I did not *know*," he said, "but I have heard people say the Wahhabis don't like what the professors are doing. They want it stopped. That man at the cafe yesterday—he looked like an Arab to me, and he was dressed expensively. What could he want from you, who have just come to Peshawar? After the cafe, your friend Rasheed said some things, until he saw I was listening and he stopped. But I had heard enough.

"When I first met you, I saw you would not go with the professors to learn about their work," Yusuf said. "You were angry with your father—and I think Rasheed saw that, too. I think he told the Wahhabis. I think they want you to help them."

I stood there listening as a silent tide of men flowed past.

"When my family came to Peshawar, we were refugees," Yusuf said. "A bad thing had happened to us, and my father knew someone who knew Professor Shaheen. The professor brought us to the hotel. They gave my father a job, then me. The professor helped us.

"Extreme people don't care about *people*," he said, his eyes flashing now, "but the professor does. He is a good man. And Pir Sahib, *he* cares about people."

I nodded. "Yeah."

Yusuf was looking at me. He was, I realized, waiting. For me to say more.

"I know I need to figure out some stuff," I said. "But don't worry. Nobody's going to make me do anything I don't want to do."

Yusuf broke into a smile. "Then please, walk with me! We are just coming to Qissa Khwani Bazaar. In your life, you must see this place."

The Street of Storytellers began as a wide boulevard full of clusters and crowds of men, its edges packed with stands and stalls, with carts of fruit and nuts and flowers. The sounds were like a mix of centuries: the *clop* of hooves, the creak of an ox cart, the blare of horns. The faces were all the ages of humanity.

"This is the famous place!" Yusuf said. Behind him the boulevard opened onto a broad, wide plaza; across it rose a tall, medieval-looking gate through which slow traffic poured and poured. Here were long, canvas-topped stands piled with pyramids of fruit—melons, oranges, bananas, mangoes, and fruits I'd never seen before. The great plaza was rimmed with open-front shops selling cloth, brass, guns, animal skins. One shop was full of ammunition; another had loudspeakers horning onto the street. Within the shade of the shops, people sat talking over pots of tea.

We came up to a parked scooter rickshaw with a painting, in color across the back, of a pink Lincoln Continental parked by the water at the bottom of Manhattan. Crowding up behind the car was the New York City skyline, with the twin towers of the World Trade Center rising into the sky.

Yusuf went up and spoke to to the driver of the rickshaw, then he motioned at me to climb in. As we pulled away, blatting out dark exhaust, Yusuf waved out at the Storytellers' Bazaar.

"You see?" he shouted over the noise. "Here is everything!"

8.

Not What I Was

IT WAS TIME. At last.

"Will you wait out here?" I asked Yusuf outside the Shaheens' gate. It was four p.m.

"No, I will come back in one hour. Then I will wait here."

I was on the porch, about to knock, when the door opened. Mrs. Shaheen stood back in the shadows. "Oh, thank God it's only you," she said. "I mean...I am very glad you have come, Luke. Please come inside. Quickly."

As I stepped in she leaned past me, looking quickly out the door. "Did you see anything outside?" she asked. "Anything strange? Unusual?"

I wanted to say, *Everything here is strange and unusual.* But I said, "I don't think so. Like what?"

"Men outside? Anyone who seemed to be watching?"

"No. I'm pretty sure no."

Mrs. Shaheen nodded. She rubbed her hands together. "I'm so sorry," she said. "We had a lovely tea planned. I'm so sorry."

"What for? Did something happen?"

She glanced nervously backward. "Come," she said. I followed her through the living and dining rooms. Into the kitchen.

It was almost dark in here, curtains drawn across the windows. Dani was sitting at a table. She didn't look up or anything. I knew I wasn't supposed to be in here, with the women of the family in their kitchen—but they were upset.

"We were going to make a lovely tea—a beautiful tea," Mrs. Shaheen said, wandering around vaguely. "We were going to make *pakora,* pastries…We even have *hame*-burger!"

"It's *ham*burger, Mor," Dani said. She smiled, but barely. I sat down across the table.

"What happened? Something happened."

Dani, staring off, nodded.

I said, "What? Tell me. Please."

"I will make tea," her mom said. "At least we can have tea." She started bustling around. I just looked at Dani. Finally, she started to talk.

"I went to school this morning, but it was closed," she said. "The gate was locked. A big lock. A lot of girls were there, looking at it. Everyone was confused. The chokidar came out. That's the…the…"

"The guard," I said.

She blinked at me. "Yes. He came out and told us our school is shut. We said, 'But why?' He said our headmistress was killed."

Silence. Dani's mom stopped, hand above the teakettle.

I said, "Killed?"

Dani nodded.

"How? When?"

"We asked. He said, 'Sometime in the night.' We said, 'Was it an accident?' He said, 'Only God knows.' But someone *does* know," Dani said. "It was not an accident."

"How do you know?"

"Because our headmistress spoke out," she said. "I go to a girls' school, of course. But ours is a private high school, I am lucky. Some of our teachers are good, and one of mine is excellent. She taught us history and civics—and she told us Islam does not require us to go about so completely covered. Our Holy Koran only says a woman must be modest.

"Our teacher said we have a right to feel the breeze on our skin. We have a right to have a career, to make our lives. She said we have *rights.*

"Then she got a letter," Dani said. "It was left in the night, slid under the front gate of her family's home. It was not signed."

"What'd it say?"

"It accused her of immoral display. *Immoral display.*"

"What's that mean?"

"There is a new law," Mrs. Shaheen said. "It says every woman teacher, and every girl in every school, must wear a *chador* in public."

"A what?"

"A chador. It's a sort of cloak."

"Is that a burqa?"

"Not quite like that," Dani said. "It's a cloth that you draw across your body, over your head, and hold across your mouth. These men said our teacher had shown her hair."

"Her *hair?*"

"Yes. They said she caused a shock of her hair to fall outside the chador, in public. They said if she 'persisted in reckless behavior,' she would be arrested.

"Our teacher showed this letter to all of us in Civics," Dani said. "She told us, 'When these men talk of reckless behavior, they mean I should stop telling you the truth. These men do not even have the courage to sign their names!'

"She gave the letter to our headmistress, who got very angry. Our headmistress has been outspoken against the mullahs and the new regime in Pakistan—and this time, she wrote a letter to the *Frontier Post.* 'We are professional educators,' she wrote. 'We will not be silenced by bullying night letters.'"

"Whoa."

"So what happened last night—this was no accident."

Mrs. Shaheen set cups of tea before us. "Our women's organization will demand an investigation," she said. "Charges *must* be brought."

Dani shrugged. Her mom said, "Tell what happened then."

I said, "Then?"

Dani reached across the table. She picked up a folded sheet of paper. "We waited for hours, at the gate," she said, "but no one else came to talk to us. No one told us anything more. So we began to go home, finally. What else could we do?

"I was walking away from the school when a rickshaw pulled up suddenly. It stopped in front of me. Someone reached out from the back and dropped an envelope."

"Where?"

"At my feet. Inside was this." She unfolded the paper, showed it to me. It was handwritten, in the strange alphabet.

"What's it say?"

"'We know who your father is,'" she read. "'We know your family.'" The page vibrated as she held it. "'Do not interfere in our business. Learn to be what you are supposed to be.'"

I stared at her. Mrs. Shaheen went to the window, pulled open a bit of curtain and peered out.

"But I don't understand," I said. "Why you?"

Dani and her mom exchanged a look.

"I also wrote a letter," Dani said. "It was also published."

"In the newspaper?"

She nodded. Then she looked up. "In our school, we are the daughters of influential men—military officers, professors, civil servants. We are a great danger to the extremists: girls who are getting an education, who know what is going on. They are saying to us, 'This is what we will do, if you do not accept *chador and char diwari.*'"

"What's *that*?"

"It means 'the veil and four walls,'" her mom said. "This is what the extremists want for all women—never to go out, except all covered. To have no life outside the four walls of home. Chador and char diwari. The extremists talk about this almost as much as they talk about jihad."

Dani just sat there.

"I will write to everyone in our organization," Mrs. Shaheen said. "We will call for justice! But…you must stay here," she said to her daughter. "For now. Even if the school reopens…"

I said, "If?"

They glanced at each other. "We don't know," Dani said. "But Mor, I can't stay hidden. It's what they want!"

"But you have to," her mother said. "For now. You must."

I said, "Does your father know?"

"Maybe not yet—but he will," Dani said. "Peshawar is a beehive. Even before the newspapers come out, everyone will know."

"Will…will the papers say what happened to you?"

"No. That sort of thing…no one speaks about it," Dani said.

"*We* will speak about it," her mother declared. "We will protest!"

A few minutes later, we were in the living room. I sat on a couch, across a low coffee table from Dani on a chair. Her mother sat at a little table across the room, furiously writing letters. Dani slumped in her chair and stared.

I couldn't stop looking at her. She wasn't like any girl I had ever known. Her mom glanced up at us; along with writing letters, I got that she was also supervising. But she was so intently into the writing that it was almost like Dani and I were alone.

Michael Jackson was singing "Beat It" on the silvery cassette player. I asked, "When will your brother come home?"

"Not till suppertime. He's with his…friends."

"The Wahhabis."

She looked up sharply. "How do you know that?"

"I talked to some people who don't like 'em. In the bazaar."

"Did you? You *are* learning fast."

"So, are people doing anything—I mean, like, to fight against those guys?"

"It's not the same guys," she said. "The Wahhabis have been coming here just recently, but we've always had our own extremists.

And now that an Islamist general has declared himself president of Pakistan, these men are seizing their chance to put the country in a stranglehold.

"Extremists always go after the women first," she said. "New laws have been passed, stripping away what rights we have—but there *is* a women's movement. My mother is active. They are resisting."

"Where is the letter?" her mom suddenly said.

Dani was startled. "Eh?"

"The letter. Where is it? I need to quote it."

"Why?"

"Because it's evidence!"

Dani shrugged, but only at me. Then she went to the kitchen, brought back the letter, set it on the writing table. Her mom nodded, went back to writing. Sitting down, Dani gave me a conspiratorial smile. It felt like a lightning strike.

"Where were we?" she asked me.

"Uh...women are resisting?"

"Oh yes! A few have won election to our National Assembly. They are working to win back the rights our mothers and grandmothers fought for. Some even say..." She hesitated.

"What?"

"They say we have the right to choose our husbands."

"You...huh?"

"This is a radical idea. Our *parents* choose our husbands."

"Always?"

"Almost always, in Pashtun country. If a boy meets a girl he really likes, he may ask his parents to make a match with her. They will say yes or no."

"Can't the boy ask the girl himself?"

"Oh, no. To have direct contact—this is forbidden."

"So how could he meet a girl? How could he know he likes her?"

Dani shrugged. "To have direct contact—that is forbidden."

"But we're having that. Sort of."

Dani shrugged. "We were friends in America. But this isn't so safe."

I finally said, "So…will your mom and dad pick your husband?"

"Yes, but I want to go to college first. I *have* to go—I want to be a teacher. Teach more girls the truth. My father believes in me, thanks to God. But what if they choose someone for my husband who is more traditional?"

"Can't you just say no? Say you won't do it."

Dani shook her head. "I liked living in America, but I am a Pashtun girl. I love my faith—Islam teaches us to be tolerant, give to the poor, be generous with guests. It teaches us to care for our family and our neighbors, respect all good people, and pray every day.

"*This* is my religion," she said, "not men who want to lock women away and then say we must be protected. That is not religion! That is boys scared of girls."

"Okay," I said. "Okay."

She looked up, bright-eyed. "Tell me about the music you like," she said. We both glanced over: her mom was deep in letter-writing.

I said, "Music?"

"Yes. You love it, yes?"

"Oh yeah."

"So tell me—I want to know more about American music. New music."

So I talked about Prince, about Springsteen. I said how the Police were recording songs about ideas, like that we're all somehow connected. I talked about something new that I liked called hip hop, that was coming out of the cities.

Dani took in everything. When I got close to what I really felt about music and started to mumble and look at the carpet, she asked about soccer. She remembered I played. I didn't want to tell her how not-good I was.

"Do people play soccer here?" I asked instead.

"Oh yes—but Pakistanis like cricket best. And badminton, we are very good at that. Volleyball is popular, because it takes little space and it's very active."

"Could you play? Do girls play?"

"Oh, no."

"I remember you didn't play in Saratoga. You didn't want to?"

"I did want to," Dani said. "But my parents said no."

"Even in America? Lots of girls play sports there."

"Yes. But they are not Pashtun girls."

I didn't know what to say. Dani looked up. "You gave me a gift," she said. "Now I have one for you."

From her pocket she drew a little box wrapped in silver paper, the flat shape of a cassette case. She glanced again at her mother, then set the gift on the table. Put her hand over it.

"In Peshawar, people are always trading cassettes," she said. "There's a lot of Bollywood music..."

"*Bolly*wood?"

She giggled. "Indian films are made in Bombay—so, Bollywood. And the extremists share cassettes of their teachers and preachers. My brother's heroes."

"I heard."

"I have a hero, too," she said. "Her name is Meena. She is a young mother, from Kabul—she is the leader of the Afghan women's movement. Meena and her friends help the mujahideen fight the Russians. They smuggle weapons, food, information, medicine over the border. But they also struggle for women's rights.

"Meena works with refugee women, in the camps," she said. "Sometimes she comes to Peshawar, to organize and raise money."

"Have you met her?"

"I have seen her. She has to do everything secretly. Her organization is called RAWA, the Revolutionary Association of the Women of Afghanistan. The leaders of the extreme mujahideen, they try to catch her. The Afghan secret police and the Russians try to catch her. The Pakistani secret police try to catch her."

"What if they do?"

"Then they will kill her. But they have not caught her yet."

"They'd *kill* her? Why?"

"Because she works for women. RAWA has started small schools in the camps, for refugee children. Women are volunteering there—even some women from educated families like ours. These schools *teach* things, like reading, history, math, chemistry, Pashto, English. So far they are not big. It's hard to get refugee families to send their girls to school.

"In the camps, the extremists call Meena and her friends lesbians and whores. They try to turn people away from the schools, so there will be only *their* schools—the ones that teach boys to hate everyone who is not what they call a perfect Muslim.

"To get money for the girls' schools, Meena has set up sewing cooperatives in the camps," Dani said. "They make our *shalwar kameez!*" She pointed at her pajamas. "Everyone here wears these."

"I noticed. That's what they're called?"

"Yes. Meena is the bravest person I know," Dani said. "She goes over the border hidden in a burqa, or disguised as an old smuggler woman. She brings back medical supplies, all she can, to help wounded fighters here. She has seizures from a childhood illness, and she knows if she is caught, she is dead. But she keeps going. She is my hero."

Dani's eyes were shining. She spoke low, under the music. "My gift is a talk Meena gave secretly, in Peshawar. I bought the cassette from RAWA. I asked a friend to make this copy for you."

"Is it in English?"

"No, sorry, it's in Pashto," Dani said. "Meena speaks only Pashto and French. But at the very end, if you fast-forward, you will find something more. Meena has written a poem—everyone who helps her group knows it. I have translated it. At the end of this tape, I recorded my translation, in English."

"So it's your voice?" *I can hear your voice? Anytime?*

Dani blushed, looked down. "Yes." She glanced again at her mom, still busy with her letters. Then Dani lifted her gift just above the low table.

I reached for it, watching Mrs. Shaheen over Dani's shoulder. My fingers took the near end of the silvery package. Dani's fingers held the other half. Michael was singing now about how some kid was not his son—and silly as that song was, I knew I would remember it for the rest of my life.

"*Never ever* touch an unmarried Pashtun girl," I heard my dad say. I kept my finger right there, holding the package at one end as she held the other. "Billie Jean" played, Mrs. Shaheen wrote, and Dani looked into my eyes. She slid the tip of her finger forward until it almost, almost touched mine.

Then she took her hand away.

Yusuf and I rode away in a rickshaw, along the streets of the new town. Up ahead, a clean white Toyota came toward us. Behind it like a posse rode several young men on motorcycles.

"Look," Yusuf said. As the Toyota went by, I saw a slim, dark-bearded man sitting very straight in the back seat. He seemed tall. The gaggle of riders followed right behind.

"That's him," Yusuf said.

"Who?"

"The new big man of the Wahhabis. The Saudi with lots of money, who talks of bigger jihad."

"Oh yeah?" I turned back, and watched Osama bin Laden's Toyota disappear around a corner.

That guy wants my dad's work burned in a fire.

What *was* I going to do? Today was Wednesday. The day of the plan was Friday. I could still do what Rashi and Amal expected me to: just leave my door unlocked. They said it would be simple. Rashi said a fatwa had to be followed.

"How come everybody talks so much about religion here?"

I blurted out. "I mean, not that it's a bad thing. But why so much?"

Yusuf nodded, thoughtfully. "To us it is the most important thing. And sometimes, it is all we have."

Back in my room, with the typing going *clack clack* next door, I put Dani's cassette in my Walkman. In the headphones I heard a woman's voice on a scratchy recording, with some background sound. Next there was applause—but muffled, like people didn't want to make much noise. Then a woman, she must have been Meena, began to speak.

Her voice was thin but strong, almost metallic. But since I had no clue what she was saying, I fast-forwarded and fiddled until I found softened clapping, the end of Meena's talk. Now there was a hiss, and a *chunk*. Then came the musical voice of my friend.

"'I Shall Never Turn Back,' by Meena," she began. Then she recited. The part that really hit me went like this:

> *These shackles on my feet I have broken*
> *I've opened the closed doors of ignorance*
> *I've said farewell to all golden bracelets*
> *O compatriot, O brother of mine,*
> *I'm not what I was*

After Dani's voice had given way to blank hiss, I stopped the player and took off my 'phones. I unlocked the door between our rooms, and knocked. The typing stopped.

"Luke, is that you? Come in!"

In his room, stuff was everywhere—messy stacks of file folders, piles of papers, and book after book. Jumbles of photos. A tilting pile of yellow, scrawled-on legal pads.

My dad and his typewriter were in the midst of it all. He looked up.

"I want to know about it," I said.

"Huh?"

"What you're doing. I need to get what it is."

His face changed. I was afraid he might hug me; I put up my hands.

"I just want to be clued in, okay? That's all."

He nodded. Then he said, "Okay. Tomorrow we're getting up early. There's a place I've been wanting you to see."

Go to that place. Pir Sahib said that. I'd been wondering what he meant.

I said, "All right."

9.
Story of the Stones

THE RUIN BELOW US was massive, like a wrecked stone castle or fort stacked in levels up the mountain's rocky slope. I saw stone platforms, empty pedestals, open stone terraces, and huge slabs that seemed to be the roofs of ancient chambers.

"Looks pretty empty, doesn't it?" my dad said. We were sitting on the stubby peak of a mini-mountain. Steep, craggy ridges ran out on both sides, like bent arms that cradled the great ruin below.

"Well, yeah."

"It's been this way for fifteen hundred years," he said. "When we walked here from the village, you could see how this is all hidden from outside view, right? We think that's what kept it from being totally demolished. But the invaders did find it eventually. They smashed it up pretty good."

"Why? 'Cause of idol worship?"

He squinted at me. "Why would you ask that?"

At our backs, the rocky slope fell steeply to the flat green valley. Down there, the road we'd come on speared back toward Peshawar.

"Rashi and his friends say you're making a big deal about idol worship."

"Do they!" My dad chuckled. Then he changed. "*Do* they?"

"Um…well…he said that at dinner," I said. "You know, that night." I had to be really careful what I told him.

He nodded. "I remember him saying that, yeah. So, okay. We don't *think* the accusation of idol worship was the main reason this civilization got destroyed. Back then the Peshawar Valley was full of treasure. It was a ripe target, a wealthy center of world trade. When violent tribesmen swept down from the far north in around 500 A.D., they found richness here beyond their imagination—statues covered in gold, stories carved on jewel-studded stone panels."

"So they grabbed all that?"

"Seems likely they took the gold and gems. But they left the stone sculptures and scenes—sometimes whole, sometimes broken or buried in the rubble. Many centuries later, that's what was found here."

"Why didn't the people here fight back?"

"Well, the civilization here was very high-level, but it doesn't seem to have been well-defended. Maybe that's too bad. They had a lot to lose."

I looked at the empty shapes. "Guess they lost it."

"Yes. But not before they gave us something the whole world knows."

"Like what?"

"Well," he said, "that's the story."

A few minutes ago as we'd climbed up broken stone steps to the ruin, three scruffy guides in dirty pajamas and ragged sweaters, who seemed to hang around here, had greeted my dad like an old friend. One of them scooped up a handful of rubble, then opened his hand to show me.

In his palm were bits of sculpture. Carved toes, part of a flower. A fragment of a man. There was a lot of broken stone in this ghostly place.

"Who are Rasheed's friends?" my dad was asking now. "Who said that about idolatry?"

"Um...Wahhabis."

"Rasheed's friends are *Wahhabis*?"

"Yeah..."

"But Wahhabis are in Saudi Arabia."

"Yeah. They came here for the war."

"My God." He shook his head. "Okay, I remember—Assad mentioned some rich Saudi that Rasheed is involved with. He said the guy's paying for young men to come here, to fight the Soviets across the border."

He was looking at me. I didn't say anything. He said, "Did you *meet* these people?"

"Well…just one guy. He was kind of hanging out with Rashi."

"And he told you this place was about idol worship?"

"No, Rashi said it."

"But you are saying Wahhabis are in Peshawar. And they know about our work."

"Well…I guess. I mean, Rashi called it that bad name, right?"

"Kafir. Yeah. But nobody mentioned Wahhabis. They're *very* extreme. In Saudi Arabia, they have a history of using violence against anyone they think has violated their intensely narrow version of Islam. So what did these guys say about our work?"

"Nothing," I said, because that was true—only Rashi had. Amal had just said I was in the brotherhood and had to keep my promise. My dad waited for me to say more, but I didn't.

"I would not be friends with those people," he finally said. "Assad is terrified that Rasheed is mixed up with them."

"Okay," I said, "but why would those guys give a crap about what *you're* doing? Everything here got smashed—how long ago?"

"About 500 A.D."

"So why do they care?"

"Because of what was *created* here. Almost no one has heard of this ruin, but people all over the world know the symbol that was born here. You know it."

"I do?"

"Oh yes—and it expresses something that religious extremists tend to really, really not like."

"Rashi says it's idol worship."

"That's what they *say*. But it's not."

He made a fist, and looked out at the huge horizon.

"This was once a place of pilgrimage that was famous, and it's important that you understand why—especially if extremists are sniffing around," my dad said. "What happened here is a great story. Assad and I think now is the time to tell it."

"Okay, but...could you give me the short version? Like, abridged?"

He grinned. "What, you don't have a few hours?"

Nope, I thought, *and neither do you. Friday is tomorrow.*

At that point, my dad stopped making sense.

"What made rock 'n' roll?" he asked.

"What?"

"Rock music. Didn't it come out of black and white music combining?"

"Well...yeah, pretty much. Electric blues and country. Elvis Presley doing songs by black guys—stuff like that."

"Right—so it was a combination. Music from different American cultures came together and made something new, right? Something powerful."

"Yeah, and it's the same with this new stuff, hip hop," I said. "In the cities, black artists are putting rhymes onto pieces of different music—jazz, funk, R&B. It's really cool."

"So when cultures and styles combine," he said, "what comes from that can be new. And amazing, right?"

"Well...I guess so..."

"So hold that thought. It's important for you to hold that thought."

But I didn't, actually. I'd been bothered by a different thought.

On the ride up here, things had gotten bad. My dad woke me up way too early, but then it was good to get out of the city. The taxi drove us along a road whose only early-morning traffic was trucks, flocks of sheep, some camels. We worked our way through a town thronged with people, then cruised along a flat planted countryside. That's when things got tense.

I hadn't meant to say it—it was stupid to say it. But it popped out.

"How come Dani's eyes are blue?"

"Pardon?"

"Well...she's Pashtun, right?"

"Yes." My dad turned from the window, to study me.

"But Pashtun people have brown eyes," I said. "Brown eyes, dark hair. I mean, hers are, like...really blue."

"Well, cultures and peoples have mingled in Peshawar for more than two thousand years," he said. "In the days before auto and air travel, people moved through this valley with huge trade caravans. So did conquering armies, even new religions. You'll see folks with broad, Asiatic faces in the city—they probably descend from the army of Genghis Khan, the conqueror who rolled across from Mongolia, above China, in the thirteenth century.

"You'll also see European features—like blue eyes," he went on. "I've seen city Pashtuns with red hair and freckles. Those traits may come from the British, who ruled India, including what's now Pakistan, for a couple hundred years. Or they may come from way back—from the soldiers who fought all the way here from Europe with Alexander the Great, three hundred years before Christ.

"So Peshawar's seen many eras of intermingling," he said. "Dani's eyes are...well, they're one product of that."

"Huh."

He studied me. "They're a fairly striking product," he said. "Those eyes."

I stared ahead.

"Luke. Is something going on?"

"Why? 'Cause I asked a question?"

"No..."

"You're a teacher, right? Don't teachers *like* questions?"

"Yes, and we also like answers. So just tell me. What's going on?"

"Nothing."

He sighed. "Luke, we talked about not putting that girl at risk. Didn't I tell you what could happen?"

"Yes, Dad. Nothing *happened.*"

"Okay, so what nothing? Tell me about the nothing, Luke."

But the driver…what about the driver? I tilted my head toward the mustached guy at the wheel. My dad froze, and grimaced. Maybe we'd already said too much. So we sat in silent tension the rest of the ride, till we came to a little dusty town and got out. We drank tea in silence in a roadside shop while boys tried to sell us stuff, chanting "Buddha?" "Buddha?" We left them behind as my dad led me on a half hour's hot, tense, dusty walk.

He was up ahead, striding across this empty-looking plain; I lagged behind, irked that he'd harassed me again about Dani. Plus, all I could see was some bare mini-mountain, up ahead on the flatness. We were walking to that? What was I *doing* here? It was hot and my feet hurt and I thought this was just stupid, until finally we came around an edge of the mini-mountain.

That's when I saw the ruin, rising inside the cradling arms.

"When people bring new things together," he was saying, "like with rock 'n' roll or this…what's it called?"

"Hip hop."

"Hip…hop?"

"Yes, Dad."

"Okay. Okay. So when cultures come together, what pushes through can be really powerful. It can even—like with a new music—spread far and wide. Think how rock has gone around the world."

"Sure."

"And if you're like Assad and me, you look for that sort of thing in history," he said. "You dig through old books and materials, even through actual ruins. You search for *some*thing—some twist or turn in the world's story that maybe hasn't really been told. That's the historian's dream, to find a story like that."

"I get that."

"Then one day, two of you find each other. One's from the West, the other from the East. You share what you've learned—and before long, a new old story starts to come through. It's been there all along, but people haven't really *looked* at it. No one has shared it in a way that could *spread*.

"The chance to do that...I mean, wouldn't that be kind of amazing?" He glanced sideways at me. "Maybe you'd throw yourself into putting that story together. You might even sort of...forget about other things."

He waited for me to say something. I didn't. So he said, waving his arm wide, "Luke, we're looking at a *lost civilization*. And we can't see it because it's hazy today, but across that northern horizon, four of the world's highest mountain ranges come together—including the Himalayas, which rise from here across the whole top of India.

"There are only a few passages through or around those mountains—northeast into China, southeast into India, and west toward Europe. So in ancient times, a huge amount of the trade and traffic that moved between those old civilizations had to pass through the Peshawar Valley. This was a *gateway*—and a meeting place."

"Okay."

"Imagine these long caravans, trudging into this valley, laden with goods and people from China, India, Persia—that's Iran, today—and from the Middle East. Even from Europe."

"They brought stories, too," I said.

"That's true! How'd you know that?"

I shrugged. "I heard it in the bazaar."

"Well...okay. So this story comes together in the first century A.D., around the time of Christ. Back then the caravans were doing a huge business—metal and wine from the Romans, silk from the Chinese, jewels and spices from India. With all the trading here, people in the Peshawar Valley became quite rich.

"Back then this valley was called Gandhara"—*Gan-DAHR-a*, he pronounced it. "Folks here built cities, libraries, universities, and places like this."

"What *was* this?"

"I'll get to that. But then around the year 100 A.D., something happened in Gandhara that hadn't happened before. Not anywhere."

"This is the short version, right?"

"Yes! Gandhara was the first place where Eastern and Western civilizations came together to make something powerful in a *creative* way—like the rock 'n' roll of its time. What came together here had meaning for people, and it spread far and wide. Just about everyone today knows it."

I tossed a little rock down the slope. I heard a scrabbling to the right. Some goats were over there, standing high up on a slope that was so shaley and steep, you couldn't imagine climbing it. I wondered how they got there. I wondered how I got here.

We sat a minute in the wide-open silence. Then my dad picked up the story.

"Alexander the Great and his soldiers came from the mountains above Greece—and after they'd conquered everything from Egypt to here, Gandhara became the eastern end of a Greek-speaking empire. For three hundred years before Christ, actually longer than there has been a United States, Greek culture and Greek kings dominated the old trading paths. From the land of the pyramids all the way to Gandhara, people were learning the Greek way of looking at life. And that was a *new way*.

"See, Greek culture was about *people*—and that was radical. You know they invented democracy, right?"

"Everyone knows that, Dad."

"Yes, and they also believed anyone could learn. So across their empire the Greeks built places of learning, called *gymnasiums*. If you wanted to get an education, discuss the meaning of life, compete in sports—the Greeks created the Olympics, right?—well, if you were a young man and your family could afford it, you could go to a gymnasium.

"All those places of learning across the old pathways taught Greek—and that *connected* people. Now the world could talk. People along those old routes were doing business, telling stories. They were sharing things that mattered to them."

I said, "Like people here trade cassettes?"

"Um…you mean tapes?"

"Yeah. People trade cassettes of music, and…like, talks. From the mosques and stuff."

"Wow—you have been learning things. And yes, back then they would have shared music along with stories. Can you imagine people from different places, sitting around their cooking fires at night, singing and talking and listening to each other?"

"Yeah." I could imagine that.

"These travelers and traders might also carry with them artwork—small carvings and sculptures, of gods and goddesses from their cultures. And the Greeks had fantastic sculptors. They were really into that stuff.

"Around this time, the Greeks started carving images of regular people—warriors and athletes, mothers and children. See, if you start to believe anyone can learn, then everyone sort of *matters*. This was a really new idea—and the power guys, the kings and priests and so forth, didn't always like it."

"Why not?"

"Well, think about it," he said. "If people can get educated, who knows how far they'll go? If anyone can compete, anyone might win! Suddenly it wasn't just the rich and powerful who might matter in the world."

I said, "Short version! Short version!"

"But that's it! Or that's *half* of what came together here. With all the money in Gandhara, there were artists working here, either Greek or Greek-trained. In this place they could earn a decent living—a rich trader might pay you to make a fine statue for one of the popular temples. And Gandhara right then had an open-minded king. He supported all this, and that's when a *second* new idea found its way here. This one came from the East—from India, along the Grand Trunk Road.

"See, Luke, ideas are *powerful*—and people who are threatened by them may strike back. Religious extremists hate the idea that got expressed in a new symbol here. They might call it idol worship. And they might try hard to wipe it out."

I got that. More than he knew. I pictured my dad's room at the hotel, full of his and Professor Shaheen's writings and notes and photos. I thought, *What if they can't get all that stuff to burn it?*

Then what will they do?

10.

Throne of the Spring

MY DAD TOSSED A PEBBLE. I watched it skitter and roll.

"The priests of the old religions had huge power," he said. "If you wanted life's mysteries on your side—if you hoped a sick child would get better, say, or a new business would succeed—you went to the temples. You gave money, offerings to the priests. People believed that only they could tap the secret sources of well-being and wisdom. Only they had the secret knowledge.

"Some priests were no doubt wise and good, and others were fakes and criminals—but many were rich, and nearly all were powerful," he said. "Then came a sort of rebellion. In northern India, one guy started to teach that there was no need to give offerings to priests—we all just needed to wake up."

"What, like people were asleep?"

"Well, in a way we still are, don't you think? A lot of what we do, we don't really understand. It's like we're too distracted to *see*. Does that make any sense at all?"

I nodded. It kind of did, actually.

"So this guy taught waking up. He taught people how to meditate, pay attention, search in themselves for what's real."

"Okay…"

"For the rest of his life, this man just traveled, teaching anyone who was interested," my dad said. "He built no temples, and he told his followers to never make images of him. No paintings, no sculptures—he didn't want to be seen as some new god, because he wasn't. He just wanted people to search in themselves. He believed if they did that honestly enough, they would find what they needed.

"So after this guy died, his wishes held for four hundred years—no images were made of him at all," my dad said. "But people preserved his teachings, they memorized them and spread them across northern India. The old-time priests didn't like it, but they couldn't stop it. People remembered this man as the one who was awake. In their language, the Buddha."

"Geez, Dad. Why not just say so?"

"Because I want you to see this fresh! And if you think about it, the Buddha's approach was a lot like the Greeks'. They believed anyone could *learn*; he said anyone could *wake up*. These were radical ideas, Luke—and often dangerous. Back then the authority figures, the kings and priests and so forth, told everyone else what to believe, what to do. They held all the power."

"So it was like being a kid," I said.

He grinned. "Yeah, if you had authoritarian parents, which you don't. Anyway, so it's the first century A.D., four hundred years after the Buddha's lifetime, and still no images of him. Now his teachings come into this valley; people here are *interested*. The Greeks were open to new ideas—that was a big part of how their culture grew and spread. And even though Greeks were no longer ruling Gandhara, their culture and their arts were still much alive here.

"Around 100 A.D., trade with Rome and Persia and China had grown to be very strong in Gandhara. This was its wealthiest time, and Buddhism had become its dominant religion. So here in this valley, the Greek idea that anyone could learn and compete *in the world* mingled with the Buddhist teaching that anyone could wake up *inside themselves*.

"Outside and inside, right? Like two kinds of music, coming together. Then suddenly, artists here began to make images of the Buddha. This was *huge*. Rich traders must have said, 'We'll pay you—go for it!' And those very first Buddhas, from Gandhara in around the year 150, are surprisingly Greek in style. He's shown as a handsome young man, in great shape like a Greek athlete, meditating or teaching in robes like a Greek philosopher. Or a Roman senator."

"Like a hybrid thing," I said.

"Exactly! So now there's a *symbol* for this idea that people can seek the truth for themselves. And with that, the idea really caught on.

"For around two centuries, Gandhara was home to a creative explosion. Thousands of Buddha images were carved in a glittery stone that's found in this valley, then in a softer stone that could be almost mass-produced. The bigger statues and scenes got set up all around Gandhara—and countless little Buddhas were carried on the caravan trails, out into the world.

"By the time the invaders destroyed Gandhara, around 500 A.D., this symbol and the idea it expressed had migrated far beyond the mountains, all the way to China. Over the centuries since, the Buddha image has spread to the rest of the world. We all basically get what it means today."

"I saw a T-shirt once, with his face," I said. "It said, 'Inquire within.'"

"Well, that's it! That's it."

"So these guys were the first to carve that?"

"No one knows for sure who carved the very first image—but the Gandharans carved it in a way that could *spread*. They gave it the Greek appeal, the realistic power. Anyway, it's a great story." He looked at me eagerly, but carefully. "Don't you think it's a good story?"

"Well, yeah but...is it really true?"

My dad tossed another pebble. "Yes. It actually is."

"So," I said, "what's *this* place?"

He nodded. "This is *Takht-i-Bahi*, 'the Throne of the Spring.' This was the biggest center of Buddhism in the valley—a place where the monks practiced meditation, and where so many new images were installed by rich donors.

"Pilgrims came from far and wide to visit Takht-i-Bahi. It must have been a staggering sight—hundreds of Buddhas and carvings of the Buddha story, some of them sheathed in gold, others festooned with jewels. It was dazzling! And then it was destroyed.

"A century or so after those northern invaders burst into this valley, some Buddhist pilgrims from China came searching for the legendary Gandhara. They found nothing here but destruction, only simple farming people left alive. And ever since, the whole North-West Frontier Province has been seen as a dangerous region.

"When the British ruled India, they never could control the frontier. But while their soldiers were fighting and dying in the hills, other Englishmen started exploring this valley. In the early 1900s, they stumbled on Takht-i-Bahi. And what they found here took them totally by surprise."

"What, like skeletons?"

"Well, not exactly." He tossed another stone. "They found statues and carvings in the rubble that were clearly Buddhist, but also looked…strangely Greek. And from those images, archeologists and historians began to piece together the story of Gandhara."

"So, okay—if it's such a good story, why isn't it famous?"

"Because of where this *is*," he said. "We're in a frontier region that's legendary for vengeance and violence. Let's just say the ruins of Gandhara have never been a tourist attraction."

He turned to me suddenly. "Can you see how *excited* we got about telling this story to the world? I mean, this is still such a key question today. *Can* people be trusted to learn and search and decide for ourselves? Or should we all just let the people who have power tell us what to think?

"This has been a huge struggle, all through the centuries since the Greeks and Buddhists broke through—and it's still going on. A lot of people will always feel safer just being given a package of answers. But others will risk their lives to say what they think and feel is true."

"It's Bob."

"Huh?"

"Bob Marley. Stand up for your rights. That's what he said."

"Okay. So you see it, right? That's why this story *matters*." He slapped the ground. "Ow," he said, picking a sharp rock out of his palm. Then he looked up at me.

"What we've tried to do, Luke—maybe it was too much. For our families. And maybe we've tried way too hard. But…can you see why it matters? Do you get it now?"

"Yeah—but I still don't get why it makes the Wahhabis so mad. And why do they call it idol worship?"

"Okay. So the one-God religions—Judaism, Christianity and Islam—all rose out of cultures where people had worshipped older images, gods and goddesses. Now that stuff was no longer okay. The new religions made it clear: if you have faith in one God, you can't also be making offerings to Apollo or some water god. Those older images got called idols, and their worship was stamped out. People could be executed for it.

"Islam is especially strict about this. Anything seen as idol worship is a grave sin," he said. "The only thing they see as worse than that is if you're in and then you back out."

I froze. "What?"

"If you're seen as betraying the faith—that's *really* bad. At least they can't say we've done that, right?"

I said nothing. He grinned. "Anyway, Gandhara's Buddha image is something different. An idol is believed to hold some special power—but this image says the power is in *you*. That you yourself can find the truth. That's still a dangerous idea, Luke. Most every religion today has extremists who say that if you don't believe their certain way…"

"Then God hates you," I said.

"Well…yeah. So if you think your crowd has all the answers, you might hate what the Gandharan image represents. And if you do, you might put out—"

"A fatwa," I blurted.

Mistake.

He was startled. "What?"

"Um...like that. Like a fatwa."

He was staring at me. "What have you heard? *Is* there a fatwa?"

"How would I know? I just heard the word, okay?"

I sat and scratched with a pointed rock. Didn't look at him. I said to myself, *You. Are. An idiot.*

Finally, my dad sighed.

"I do need to take some more photos while we're here," he said. "Want to come walk around with me?"

"In a minute. I...kind of want to hang here for a minute."

"All right then. Come down when you're ready."

Alone now, I looked around. It was beautiful. The goats were silhouetted on that sharp ridge against the sky. On the other side, rock piles and markers stood high like watchmen. All around, you could see for so many miles.

It was quiet. Peaceful. I heard only the circling of a plane, the chirping of birds, the buzz-by of a fly. The huffing of someone coming up.

It was the oldest of the scruffy guides, climbing in a patched commando sweater. From his hand dangled a small cloth bag. He sat down beside me, nodded, and opened it.

He took out an old-fashioned matchbox, and opened that. Inside were copper coins, not quite round and very old. One had a soldier on an elephant. Another had what looked like a king. I smiled; I didn't know what to say. A goat bleated.

The old guy took out a crumpled wad of newspaper. He unwrapped it and, one after another, drew out little objects. He showed me flat stones with legs on them, pieces of carved bodies. I shrugged. He brought out the small stone head of a young Buddha, with open eyes. He showed that, then put it back in its scrap of newspaper.

"Wait," I said. I pointed. He brought the Buddha back out.

The head, about the size of a baby's fist, had lost its nose—but it did kind of look like a young Greek god, chiseled from glittery stone. The guide set it down. I looked at him. He held up two fingers.

I said, "Two...dollars?"

He shook his head. "Rupees," he said. Pakistani money. I had some.

I said, "Two rupees?" He shook his head again. I took out two ten-rupee notes. About two dollars. I held them up. He nodded.

If wondered if this was okay, but I gave him the twenty rupees. He wrapped the Buddha head back up in newspaper and gave it to me. I put it quickly in my pocket. He wrapped up the other pieces, put them back in his bag. He stood and shook my hand.

"Your father is *good* man," he said. Then he started back down.

Before long, I came down the slope. My dad was talking with the two younger guides, down there in the ruins. They both looked up at me, and smiled widely.

"I've told them you're my son," my dad said. "They're excited to meet you."

"You speak the language?"

"Pashto? Just a little. Okay, so this is Malik. This is Abdul Aziz, and this veteran gentleman coming around the corner"—the old guy—"is Muhammad Zakir. They pick up a rupee here and there from the few visitors who come to see this place."

The guides all shook my hand. "Hello!" said Malik.

"Welcome," said Abdul Aziz. "*As salaam aleikum.*"

I looked at my dad.

"That's the Muslim greeting," he said. "It means 'Peace be upon you.' You answer, '*Wa aleikum as salaam.*'"

"What's that mean?"

"'Peace be upon you, too.'"

I said it the best I could, and now the guides were leading me around to see this place's empty alcoves, its small platforms and broken pedestals, all made of gray stone. Malik took me over to a stone arcade that held broken chunks of columns, like from Greek temples. He scooped up another handful of rubble; when he opened his hand, I swear I saw bits of bone.

"Well," my dad finally said, "we should head back. Pretty cool place, huh?"

"Actually...yeah."

I touched my pocket, felt the small but heavy thing that was in there. I felt almost like it was telling me something. Or maybe this whole place was telling me something.

On the drive back we were both quiet. It was just midday; I looked out my window, at the green passing fields. An old man stood quietly by the road holding a chicken, the chicken as meditative as the man.

I still wasn't sure what to do, but I was sure about one thing. When we got back, I was going to talk to Yusuf. We would figure something out.

Because if I could help it, Rashi and his friends were not going to get their hands on anything.

PART TWO

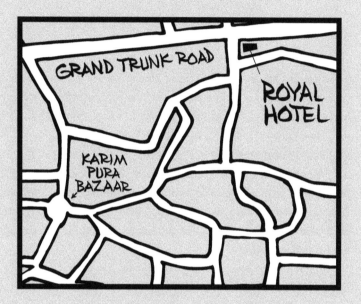

11.

Serious Business

THREE DAYS AGO, after our plane from New York had landed in Pakistan, my dad led us onto a train in a big station in a crowded and noisy city called Rawalpindi. The train was short and had lots of windows, plus two engines up front. It needed both engines, my dad said, to pull us up the hills to Peshawar.

We had rolled out of the station and were tracking across green, flat country with villages and farms when a man who'd been sitting up front got up and came back toward us. He was clean-shaven and had on a white V-neck sweater, like for tennis. He sat behind us. After a bit, he said something.

"That fellow I was sitting with," he said, kind of softly. "I think he is a lover of cheap scent."

"Hmm?" said my dad, who was reading, of course.

"Scent. Cologne." The man looked at me. "He seems to love it. Myself, not so much."

"Huh," my dad said.

The train climbed and twisted over a rocky high place, then came down toward a river that rushed blue-green between steep rocky sides, with a heavy fort up above. We crossed a steel bridge and climbed and climbed, the engines winding high, and now we were in a badlands.

All around us was steep, stony barrenness. On ridges high above stood bits of old fortifications, like teeth and broken spines. Tracking beside a twisty road, we passed a statue of a rifle bullet. Like ten feet tall.

"Pashtun country," the man in the sweater said to me. "We have crossed into the North-West Frontier Province."

"Whoa," I said.

"Yes. Behind is the Punjab, a land of farmers. Different people."

"Was there fighting here?"

"Sure—but long ago, in the British time. Now they fight over the border, in Afghanistan. And in the mountains along the border."

"Aren't these the mountains?"

"No, these are the hills. Ahead is the Peshawar Valley, then the mountains. You are going to the city?"

"Yeah."

"Very good. People will welcome you there."

"Are you sure?"

"Yes, sure. You will see."

We passed a collection of tiny huts. Dozens, maybe hundreds, of them stretched back into the distance. Close to the tracks a small boy turned in a circle, keeping in the air a little, white, wavering kite.

"Refugees," the man said.

"From Afghanistan?"

"Yes."

"Are there more?"

"Yes—so many. In Pakistan, two million."

"Whoa."

"Yes."

At last the train leveled off, and we clacked past green fields edged by orange-speckled trees. I had never seen orange trees before. When we stopped at a village station, the men who got on wore simple clothes and had faces like hawks. Some wore a flat wool hat, with a rolled edge all around.

My dad said, "See that hat, Luke?"

"Yeah…"

"You'll see it a lot. Alexander the Great brought it here, 330 years before the time of Christ."

I didn't want to hear this. I had decided on the plane: no ancient history. None.

"Alexander came from the mountains above Greece," my dad said. "He and his army fought all the way from there to that river we just crossed. That was the Indus."

"Dad."

"His soldiers wore that hat. To keep warm."

"Dad."

"People here still wear it. This is mountain country, too."

"*Dad.*"

"Huh?"

"Enough. Okay?"

"Well, I think it's interesting."

"Of course you do."

He sighed, looked sad, and went back to reading. The man in the tennis sweater leaned forward.

"We call the hat a *pakol,*" he said to me. "Your father is knowledgeable."

I shrugged. "He's a professor. He lectures."

"What is his subject?"

"History."

"So have you come for the history?"

"He has."

"And you?"

I shrugged. "I haven't come for anything."

"Not for narcotics?"

"What?"

"Narcotics. Western people sometimes come here for drugs."

"Huh. Well, not us."

"Perhaps," the man said, still softly, "your father deals in artifacts."

"Artifacts?"

"Ancient artwork. Bits of statues. There once a great civilization in this valley. There is some trade in artifacts."

"I'm…pretty sure that's not his thing. He's just writing a book."

"Ah. Interesting."

"Maybe."

"It is not permitted to deal in artifacts," the man murmured.

"Okay."

He was quiet. Then he sat back and said, "You will like Peshawar. You will find the people here are very honest. Very true."

"Huh."

The train slid into a dark, busy city station and wheezed to a stop. My dad said, "This is it!"

Everyone stood and began pulling down luggage. The man in the sweater handed me a business card. "I have enjoyed our chat," he said. "If I can be of any help while you are in Peshawar, please contact me."

I looked at the card. It said:

> *Shabbir Ahmad*
> *Prosecuting Sub-Inspector*
> *Peshawar City Police*
> *Phone no. 73128*

When I looked back up, he had stepped off the train.

Now, back from the ruin late Thursday afternoon, I was in my room. My dad had gone to meet Professor Shaheen at the museum, and I was looking through my cassettes when someone knocked.

At the door was Yusuf. With an envelope.

"This has come for you. A rickshaw driver has brought it."

"Um…thanks." I saw the neat handwriting, and tried to look calm.

He said, "Will you come down? For tea?"

"Sure. Just give me a minute."

"Of course."

I stood waiting. He glanced at the envelope in my hand.

"All is well?"

"Oh, sure."

"Yes. Good." But he didn't seem sure. "Then I will go." He backed up a step.

"Right. Fine. See you in a few."

"In a…"

"I'll be down in a few minutes," I said as I softly closed the door.

> *My parents are very worried. My mother is still writing letters. I think it's funny—writing a letter is what got me into this trouble.*
>
> *I must decide what to do. I can't be trapped here. But Luke, we can't have any more contact at all. Things are far too dangerous right now. People are watching.*
>
> *Thank you for the music, again and again. I am so glad we had our talk. May God be with you always.*
>
> *D*

Nothing more.

I stood there staring, holding the note. There was another knock.

I expected Yusuf again—but it was Rasheed.

"Hey, bro," he said. "We need to talk."

"Uh…

Rashi stepped past me into the room. He sat on my bed and watched as I walked over to the bureau and, casually as I could, slipped Dani's letter into the top drawer. Rashi had some kind of paper in his hand, too. I said, "What's up?"

"Don't joke with me, okay? Tomorrow's the day. You're still in, I know you are. You're with us."

"What?"

"You're *with* us, Luke. God has guided you. You may not know it completely in your heart yet, but you're one of us. You can't go wrong."

"Um…hey, Rashi, about that…"

"I brought you this," he said, holding out his paper. "It'll help you."
It was a pamphlet. The green cover had the drawing of a mosque behind two crossed swords. It said *Jihad in Islam,* with a quote from the Koran:

> *Those who believe fight in the cause of Allah,*
> *and those who reject Faith fight in the cause of Evil.*

Rashi pointed. "This is by a Pakistani guy, Maududi—he's famous! And it really is that simple. We're not doing anything for ourselves. We only do what God wants."

"How do you know what God wants?"

"It's right here! This is for justice in the world."

"What about women?"

"What about women?"

"When do they get justice?"

Rashi's forehead wrinkled. "They already have it, bro. Inside the home, they are like queens. Ask any good Muslim woman—she will tell you she is happy."

I thought, *Why don't you ask your sister?* But I wasn't about to mention Dani. Instead I picked out *Exodus* from the cassette case.

"How about this guy? He speaks the truth, if you ask me. Lots of people think so."

"But he can't, see? Because he's not Muslim. You'll get it, Luke, you just have to study. Let the truth come into your heart."

"Bob sings about God," I said. "He calls him *Jah.* Here, let me play—"

"No! That is *not* the name of God. Anyone who gives God a false name is a kafir. Bro, you need to get rid of this. Here, let me..."

He snatched at the tape; I yanked it back. "I don't think so, Rashi."

"Look, we're on the same team, okay?"

"No, man. We're not."

His eyes widened. "Don't *say* that. You can't say that."

"I just did say that."

"Just…tomorrow, leave your door unlocked. All right? That's all you have to do."

"I don't have to."

"You *do*. Luke…sometimes we have to do things. People who know, they tell us. There's a fatwa."

"I don't care what there is—I don't have to do something because someone else tells me." I crossed my arms. "I'm American."

"Do you believe in justice? You believe in peace?"

"Everyone does! Don't start that stuff with me, Rashi."

"Luke, this is the only way—believe me. Don't go back on what you said. You don't have to *do* anything; just forget to lock the door."

He stood up. We faced each other.

"Read the pamphlet, okay?" Rashi forced a smile. "It's a gift from me to you." He stuck out his hand. I did not shake it.

"Tomorrow," he said. "See you at lunch. Everything will be ready."

He nodded. Went to the door. Then turned back.

"We're doing this for our families," Rashi said. "It's the only *peaceful* way."

Then he was gone.

A few men were at the tables in the dining room. Yusuf came up as I sat down.

"You would like qawa?"

"No tea right now, thanks. I need to talk with you."

He nodded. "Here?"

"Not here. Can you come to the room?"

"Sure, if I bring tea."

I had to smile. "Okay."

"Qawa?" He was smiling, too. Good to have a friend.

"Absolutely. Thanks."

Upstairs, when the soft knock came, I let him in. He set the tray on the desk. I waved at the chair.

"Please. Have a seat." He did, and I told him.

I explained about the plan, as simply as I could—told him what the Wahhabis wanted me to do. He nodded when I said there was no way I was doing it. When I said Rashi told me I couldn't back out, he frowned.

"I can't tell my dad," I said. "This book means everything to him—how can I tell him I even talked with those guys about stealing it? And I can't tell Professor Shaheen his own son is betraying him. I'm pretty sure he has no idea—and I couldn't do that to him, you know?"

Yusuf nodded.

"Rashi said this is the only peaceful way," I said. "But I can't. I won't. So, I mean...now what?"

Yusuf was thinking. "You said there is a fatwa. It came from Sheikh Osama."

"That's what Rashi said."

"Then I think Osama is testing his power. This is his first fatwa."

"How do you know that?"

"In Peshawar, everyone hears things," he said. "The leader of that group is a Palestinian, Sheikh Azzam, who gives many talks about the mujahideen. He is the one who calls the fight against the Russians a holy war."

"I heard about him," I said. "He says the holy warriors can't die, but then birds sing when they go to heaven."

"That's him, he tells these stories. People are sharing cassettes of his talks."

"I've heard that."

"Yes—and Sheikh Azzam gave a big fatwa," Yusuf said. "He said believers must come to Peshawar from all Muslim countries, to join the rebels. Sheikh Osama came, but until now he has only given out money. If he has issued a fatwa, I think he is trying out his power. That is new."

"Okay..."

Yusuf sat, thinking.

"The professor's son has promised these men you will cooperate," he finally said. "He does not want to lose face—that is bad for a Pashtun. And in the bazaar, we are starting to laugh at these Wahhabi guys. People say they don't fight, they only play at being mujahideen. They won't want to look bad over this."

We both sat there a minute.

"These are extreme people," he said. "This is serious business."

"I guess." Then I remembered something. "Wait a second."

I unzipped the front pocket of my backpack. It was still there. A small white card.

"I met a cop. On the train. He said if I needed help, I could call him. See the number?"

He studied the card. "But...this is the police."

"Oh, you're quick."

"But this is Pakistan. Here police cannot always be trusted."

"Well, this guy seemed decent—and we have to do something. Let me just call him."

Yusuf nodded, slowly, then stood up. "There is a phone downstairs."

"Will you get in trouble? Aren't you supposed to get back to work?"

"This is quiet time. Quick—follow me."

An hour later we were sprinting across the Grand Trunk Road, through a fast-closing break in the traffic. We were headed for the Government Transport Service bus station, a drab-looking building all the way across the intersection from the Royal.

"This is a good place to meet," Yusuf yelled over the noise as we reached the other side. "Everyone comes here! No one will notice." I was trying to figure *that* one out as I followed him in.

The terminal was plain, clean and echoey inside. I could see blue buses, undecorated, sitting out back. We bought milky tea at a stand, and sat on a bench. We waited.

"Maybe he won't come," I said.

"He said he would come. I think he will."

After a few long minutes, Sub-Inspector Shabbir Ahmad strode up in a pressed white shirt and creased khaki trousers. He shook my hand, then Yusuf's, addressing him in Pashto. "Come with me," he told us in English.

He led us to a closed door in back that was guarded by a cop with a twirled-up mustache. The cop saluted the inspector, and pulled open the door to a small, windowless room. It had a beat-up table and chairs.

The inspector motioned for us to sit, then sat at the head of the table. He said, "Tea?"

"We just had some, thanks," I said.

He nodded. "Tell me what is the problem."

I told him, carefully, what we'd decided to tell. That there was a plan to break into my father's hotel room. That I'd been pressured to help.

"How?"

"How was I pressured?"

"No. How would you help?"

"By leaving my room door unlocked tomorrow, when we go out to lunch. There's another door between our two rooms. The lock for that one's on my side, with a key."

He nodded. "Why would someone want to do this? Are there valuables in your father's room?"

"No—it's about a project. A book. I..." Suddenly I felt lost.

"They are Wahhabis," Yusuf said quickly. They said something in Pashto. The inspector asked a question; Yusuf answered.

The inspector said, "We don't need something like this in Peshawar right now."

"I can't let it happen," I said. "I can't let them steal my dad's work."

"For whom *does* your father work?"

"Um…he's a professor. At a college in the U.S."

"*Ah-cha*. I remember, you said this on the train. But in Peshawar—for whom does he work here?"

"I…guess he works for himself. I mean, he's writing a book."

"But why has he brought *you* here?" He leaned forward, his eyes drilling into mine. Suddenly I felt we'd made a mistake. It was stuffy in here. Too hot.

"Wh…what do you mean?"

The inspector shrugged. "Isn't it possible that your father could be collecting more than historical information? Having his son with him could serve as a good cover."

"For him?" It took a second for this to sink in. "My dad's not a *spy*."

Again he shrugged. "We have all manner of foreign agents here. Every one pretends to be something else."

"But not my dad, see? He's writing a book, with a professor from the university here. It's about the Buddhists. The statues."

The inspector nodded. "The artifacts. We discussed this on the train."

"Yeah, but he's not *stealing* them. He studies them."

I felt a little clench of fear. Back in the room, my Buddha head was in the top drawer. If the cops went searching…

"Have you seen our city museum?" he suddenly asked.

"Uh…no. Not yet."

"You should go. The artworks there are great treasures of the world."

"But…but the jihadi guys say it's idol worship. And there's a fatwa," I said, trying to get this back on track. "They say they have to stop the professors' book. My dad's room is full of the project—pictures, files, everything they've written. They want to steal it, and burn it all up. They *told* me that."

The inspector nodded. Thought. Then he spread his hands, palms on the table.

"We are able to make contact with this group. We don't need them creating an incident like this, especially one involving an American. We will let them know the hotel will be watched, not to try anything. I will arrange for a detail, plainclothes. What are your room numbers?"

I told him.

"Fine. Good. No one will disturb these rooms until you come back, at what time?"

"I don't know—two? Three at the latest."

"All right. It's a good place, the Royal. Nothing bad will happen there tomorrow." He stood up. "If there's nothing else…"

"No—that's it." I stood, and shook his hand. "Thank you."

"Of course. But, young man. These people are not going to be happy with you."

"Yeah, well…"

"How soon can you leave the city?"

"I don't know. It's up to my dad."

"Of course. Well…after this, if anyone threatens you or if you notice anything that seems out of the ordinary, you must call me."

"Okay, yeah." *Out of the ordinary,* I thought. *That's pretty much everything.*

"Do you still have my card?"

"I…think so." I slipped two fingers into my back jeans pocket. "Yep."

"All right then," he said, and he walked out of the room.

When we got outside the terminal, I stopped and took a deep breath. The air was blue with exhaust fumes, but I didn't care.

"Whoa," I said.

"We usually stay away from the police," Yusuf said.

"I can sort of see why."

12.
Night of Song

BACK IN THE ROOM, I opened the top drawer in the dresser. In a little clear area alongside my socks and underwear, I'd put the Buddha head, Rashi's pamphlet, Dani's Meena cassette, her invitation to tea...and her letter.

I pulled that out. Read it again. I couldn't talk with her again? Not *ever*?

I didn't want to make any more trouble for her; we both had enough to worry about. But I couldn't help thinking that the one person who could really help me think through this situation...was her.

And our families were *friends*. I had been to her house—to both her houses, in America and here.

What would be so wrong with us just talking?

Just before dinner, a letter came from my mom. She didn't have any news, so she carefully described the Christmas lights in town, the music in the stores, the holiday concert she went to with the boyfriend. It was like a perky update from another planet.

Assad came to the hotel with my dad for dinner. I ordered chicken. I had decided that if I always ordered chicken, for lunch and for dinner, I couldn't be served anything too weird.

"So you enjoyed Takht," Assad said.

"Actually, yeah. It was something."

"Oh, it is that. Next I would like to be your guide at *my* favorite place. Our wondrous city museum."

"I've...heard of that."

"Yes, I believe I did mention it," Assad said. "You must let me give you a tour. Tomorrow, Friday, is our sabbath. Perhaps Saturday morning?"

"Oh...um, sure."

"Luke? You okay?" my dad asked.

"Yes. Why?"

"I don't know...you seem preoccupied."

"I'm fine. Hey, food!"

Yusuf had come up with a full tray. He served each of us, then he said to Assad, "We have visited Pir Sahib. Luke is invited to the dargah."

Assad lit up. "Why, that's fantastic! You must go. And tonight, Thursday evening, is *the* night."

"What's this?" my dad asked.

"It's the shrine of Rahman Baba," Assad said.

"Oh sure, the shrine. And Luke was invited?"

"You do not need an invitation," Assad said to me. "Anyone can visit our shrines. Each shrine in Pakistan is dedicated to the memory of a famous *Sufi*, a wise and spiritual man. Rahman Baba was our greatest Pashtun Sufi, a poet *and* a saint. His shrine is very special. On Thursday evenings especially, people go there to relax, pray, have food if they are hungry, and hear music. Do you like music?"

"Hey, Luke loves music!" my dad said before I could answer. "But ...is this place safe?"

"Oh, no place could be safer," Assad said. "Anyone can come, of any faith, men and women both. The shrine of Rahman Baba is the most peaceful spot in Peshawar. Except, perhaps," he said to me, "for our museum."

"Well," my dad said. "All right then."

"In a little while, I will be finished—I will come for you," Yusuf said to me. "We must take a rickshaw. It is just outside the city."

"Okay, I guess," I said. "Is the music good?"

Yusuf smiled. "I think you will tell me."

Well, I thought, *it'll keep my mind off things.*
I hope.

I wondered if I should hide the Buddha. In the drawer, I had set it on a little nest I'd made by crumpling up newspaper, the way the old guy on the mountain had wrapped up his treasures.

The stone head's eyes were open, almost like he was looking up at me. I didn't know where else to put him, so I left him there. I unfolded Dani's letter and laid it over the Buddha, like a little tent. If someone took a quick look, that might hide it.

Carefully, I closed the drawer.

Folded into a scooter rickshaw, we rode swaying and bumping out of the city, in the early evening when the light was soft and getting low. We snaked our way through the alleys; then their squeezed-together world of sagging wood, brick and tin fell behind and we were in dusty, earth-colored outskirts. Everything almost glowed in the low, slanting light. Men clustered outside tiny shops. We passed homes with rounded walls of earth and straw, then patches of deep green... and now a big, uneven field full of small piles of stones.

Hundreds of these piles.

"Is this a *graveyard?*"

"Yes. Muslim graveyard."

"Aren't people, like, buried in the ground?"

"Sure. The stones mark the grave."

Up ahead, in the dimming light, I could see a grove of trees. It looked like an oasis.

"It is the dargah," Yusuf said. "The shrine."

It *was* an oasis. Looking in among the trees, I saw deepening shadows and yellow flickering light. Along its edge out here, men sat in the shade smoking cigarettes on the rude beds I'd been seeing in Peshawar, often outside shops. Each bed had a frame and legs of rounded wood, with a tight-woven mesh of thin rope to lie or sit on. Past the beds and the loitering men, a neat-swept path led between thick trees that had wide pale trunks, fat dusty leaves, and a whole chorus of birds.

The birds were somewhere up there... or everywhere up there.

"Many birds are living here," Yusuf murmured when I looked up. "The saint was so gentle he could talk to the animals. When anyone has a bird that is sick, they bring it here, to live and get better."

"Huh."

Within the grove we came to a scatter of small, white brick buildings. In the middle was the saint's tomb, a long box of shiny marble set on a pedestal inside a tall screen of curlicued metal. The screen had folded pieces of paper stuck into it, and many tied-on bits of colored cloth.

"What're all those?"

"Wishes. People believe the spirit of the saint can ease a suffering, heal a child. We come here to be with him."

"So he's... like a god?"

"No, a wise and gentle man. He is a pathway to God."

"But everyone here's Muslim, right?"

"Yes, but in this place it does not matter your belief," he said. "If you are hungry, you can eat. See?"

He waved over to the side, and I saw big cooking pots steaming under the wide-spreading trees. "Men who live here, we call them *faqirs,* they are religious men who travel among the shrines," he said. "They serve food and tea to anyone who needs."

Long-bearded guys in colored robes moved among the pots. Things were painted in the different alphabet, in green on the sides of the small white buildings.

"What's on those walls? Words?"

"Yes. From the poems. When Pashtun people have trouble, maybe they are confused or sad, our tradition is to meditate on the problem, then open the poetry of Rahman Baba. Just open to any page. If they were helped by the poem, people can pay to have the line they found in the book painted on these walls."

"Have you done that?"

"Myself, no. But I have looked at the poems."

Around us were regular-looking men, in pajamas and vests and sandals. They sat on the rough beds, they prayed at the screen of the tomb, and—I could see now—they waited to speak with someone who sat on the deep porch of the widest low building. In those shadows, I saw...

"Hey!"

"Yes. Pir Sahib has given a talk. Now people can ask for advice, or a blessing."

Torches glimmered at the edges of the porch. Pir Sahib sat on a cushion, talking with a man. I could see his white beard and nodding head, then his brilliant smile.

"So, like...is he a saint, too?"

Yusuf shrugged. "He is a teacher. If you study with him, you have to work really hard. The Sufis that teach, we call them Pir."

"Can...can anyone get in line?"

"Of course!"

So I went over. As the shadows got deeper and more torches were lit around the courtyard, I stood and waited. It was like a place outside time. When my turn came and I bent to sit, Pir Sahib's face lit up.

"You have come!"

"Yeah. I mean yes," I said, folding myself onto the cushion. "Thank you." I didn't know what to say, really.

"Have you given your father's shoes a good test?"

"Well...kind of. I went with him to this place that he studies, and I mostly get it now, what he's doing. I get why it's important. But..."

He smiled. "This is good," he said. "This 'but'."

"Um...it is?"

"Yes, it can lead us to your question." He held out his open hand, like he was inviting me, or welcoming me. "What *is* your question?"

"I just wonder…what can *I* do? I mean…" A wave of feeling hit me, like heat. "How can I not make things worse?" My voice cracked. I was embarrassed.

"Good!" He leaned forward, put his hand on mine, and I was calm. Peaceful again.

"This is a very good question," Pir Sahib said. "To know what we can do, we must learn to be who we are. Can you live from your own true heart? Can you walk through this world as yourself?"

I looked up. His eyes were searching now, serious. "This takes courage," he said. "I see that in you. When the music begins, only to listen. Inshallah, you will hear something just for you."

"Um, okay. Inshallah."

I wasn't sure what to think. He sat back, smiling at me gently, and I knew that was it. I'd had my time with the teacher. I didn't want to go, but I stood up, and made an awkward bow.

"Thank you," I said.

Pir Sahib nodded, his eyes warm on mine.

And he smiled.

"Was that good?" Yusuf had waited in the deepening shade of a tree.

"I…yeah. It was."

"Did he tell you a joke?"

"A joke?"

"He does that sometimes. He loves to laugh."

"Well…God, I don't know," I said, because I really didn't.

Then I heard the musicians.

The squeaky sound of tuning up came from the other side of the tomb. Men were going over there. There were only men.

"I thought women could come here, too," I said as we walked over.

"Yes, but in daytime. If you see women here, you must not look at them."

"Why not?"

He shrugged. "People would not like it."

The musicians were sitting under a broad-spreading tree, getting ready with their instruments. Men around me sat down on the ground, and on rough beds around the edges. Torchlight played over them and on the players. One player sat behind a wooden box that, as I came closer, I saw had a yellowed old keyboard. With one hand he worked a sort of accordion bellows at the back, and the thing gave out a wheezy, tuneful sound.

Another guy had a stringed instrument like a strange old violin. Another had something like a clarinet. Two guys sat with drums that were dark wood cylinders lying sideways on their laps, with skin at both ends tightened by cords. I thought of that *Star Wars* scene where the alien band is playing weird instruments in the interplanetary bar, but these were skinny men in white pajamas and green caps.

The boxy thing wheezed into loud sound. The guy with the strange violin plucked out deep-banjo notes, and the drummers started pocking and thumping.

The drums...were interesting.

I looked closer. Each drummer had one hand going fast now at his drum's narrow end, ticking out notes while at the wider end his other hand thumped a low groove. As the music grew, the drummers built and built the rhythm...

And it *rocked*.

The sound kept developing as the men around me rocked and swayed—and when it was really cooking, as the drums percolated and the instruments wheezed and wailed, a new guy in bright white pajamas and a fancy vest came out and he was the singer. He sat on a cushion in front of the players. He closed his eyes and started swaying, then singing—and now everyone clapped as the music kept building, rising and falling but building all the time. The drums interwove and drove it as they pocked and rocked, and I was more and more into it...

And then something wasn't right.

People were looking to the side. A bunch of young men were coming through the trees. They marched to the edge of the crowd and stood there, looking all pissed off. Most of them had beards and they all glared at the musicians. At the edge of the lamplight I saw Rashi. I didn't see Amal. At the back of this bunch, some guys were holding up long sticks, like clubs.

The music faltered. It slowed, wheezing...then it stopped.

Some of the men who'd been sitting on the ground, listening, got up and went over, hands out in a welcoming way—but the newcomers weren't having it. They wouldn't shake hands. They gestured angrily at the musicians and said stern, high, angry things. Someone shouted, "An offense to Allah!"

That upset the men in the audience. Now there was talking all around me, with confused looks and shaking of heads. Nobody was happy. Rashi locked eyes with me. He looked at me for a long moment, then turned away. They all did—they just turned and walked off through the shadows. There was murmuring and muttering as everyone here watched them go.

"Has this happened before?" I said to Yusuf. "Here?"

"No—I don't think so. It is not good. This is a sacred place. A peaceful place."

The men who'd tried to welcome the Wahhabis returned to the crowd, kind of shrugging as everyone talked. People were trying to work out what had happened, you could see it all around; then the music started again. It quickly built back up, and again we were pulled into the singing and the wheezing and wailing of the instruments. The drums were pocking and rocking and I almost forgot about almost everything—about the Wahhabis, about what would happen tomorrow, about my dad and protecting the project...about almost everything but her.

The music only made my feelings about her come up stronger. But still I got kind of lost in listening, not understanding what the singing meant but definitely getting its really strong emotion. The drums pocked and rocked and we all swayed together until, suddenly, it was over. The song, or the jam or whatever, was over.

A few people stood and went up to the players, tossing out rupee notes that fluttered down around them. I went up, too. One of the drummers looked up at me. I said, trying to remember: "Salaam... um, salaam..."

"You say, 'As salaam aleikum,'" the drummer said. He had a roundish, open face and a thick mustache and he smiled at me, like this was the latest good surprise in a life of good surprises.

"As salaam aleikum," I repeated.

"And I say, 'Wa aleikum as salaam.'" He stuck out his hand. "I am Wasil. Call me Wasi."

We shook. "I'm Luke."

"Look?"

"Yeah. So, hey." I pointed at his drum. "How do you *play* that?"

13.

Day of Prayer

FRIDAY MORNING.

Oh crap.

The old typewriter clacking woke me up. I knocked on the door between our rooms. He didn't answer, still clacketing. So I pounded.

"Ah…yeah! Luke? Come in!"

It was ridiculous in there. His desk was piled thick and high with papers, photos, files and notebooks that almost buried his typewriter, a pale-green metal portable. More of the project was in piles on his bed, on the floor. Everywhere.

"Man," I said. "How do you sleep?"

"Sleep?" He grinned. "What's that?"

"Isn't Friday, like, the Muslim sabbath? No work?"

"Well, people do sometimes work on Friday, after midday prayers. But hey, not us—we're due to head out for lunch at one. Think you can occupy yourself till then?"

I didn't answer.

But actually there wasn't much to do. Yusuf was working. I'd gone outside to stand out front, and the intersection was almost… well, not *quiet,* but much lower-key. Friday was different, here.

Most of the morning I listened to music. I looked out my window, down at the alley. No one walked by. I opened the drawer and read her letter again. I looked at the Buddha. He looked back at me. I wondered: *Will she come to lunch? Are they letting her go out at all?*

I picked up the Buddha and held him. He was carved of dark gray stone, small but heavy, with little glitters. He'd been broken off in back from some larger sculpture, and over the centuries he'd lost the front of his nose—but still he was so well made that he seemed almost alive. Like he was looking up at me.

Then I saw that moisture from my palms had seeped into his stone, turning him a little black around the back. Quickly I put him back in his newspaper nest.

Idiot. The thing sits forgotten for fifteen hundred years, then YOU get it and start messing it up.

Had I messed up everything? What was going to happen?

I didn't know. I couldn't know.

I put the music back on. I thought about last night, how Wasi had showed me a little of how to play the two-headed drum. I forgot what he called the drum, but I remembered that I liked how it sounded—*dum POCK, dum POCKA dum POCK*—and how the music built all around it while the rhythm kept on coming through. In my head, I heard it now.

At noon, Yusuf came up with tea on a tray. I hadn't asked for it. He said, "How are you?"

"A little nervous. Mostly bored."

"Then come."

He led me up to the third floor, and from there to a cramped, narrow stairway. In darkness at the top, Yusuf unlocked a door and pulled it open—and now he was a black silhouette, stepping into light. I followed, unfolding myself upward through the hatch.

We were on the roof. In bright sunshine. "What about this?" Yusuf said, waving at the all-directions view.

"Nice!"

Old Peshawar was a low jumble, all brown and white and tan. Here and there, minarets—the little towers alongside the mosques, where loudspeakers broadcast the call to prayer I'd been hearing every morning early—stuck up like pointy-topped candles. Beyond them rose the brown border mountains, and the pale blue sky.

We stood for a moment, looking. Then I was startled by a sweeping motion, low and white, somewhere down among the buildings.

"It is Friday prayers," Yusuf said. "All the men come to the mosque. Can you see?"

"Huh! Yeah."

Massed men in white had filled a square that was open to the sky, within the walls of a mosque. They all swept upward now, a white wave—and there was another one, over at another mosque. And a third, way over there.

"All pray together," Yusuf said. "At Friday prayers, all Muslim peoples are one. But I must go, I am working. You can stay if you like."

"Okay. Thanks."

He started to go down. Then he said, "Are you worried?"

"Maybe a little. You think the cops will be here?"

"Yes, I think—but it does not matter. No one will get into the rooms."

"Really?"

"Yes."

"How can you be sure?"

"Because you are my guest. I have given my word."

I nodded. I was coming to understand what that meant.

After Yusuf left, I stood looking out at the mountains and sky, at the jumble of rooftops and minarets and mosques, at the dense white squares of men all praying down there, and over there, and over there too.

Dean's Hotel was where people would meet in the old British Empire time—that's what Assad told us. "Everyone from generals to scalawags and secret agents," he said happily when he met my dad and me at the door. He led us into the dining room, where Dani and her mom sat quietly in silky headscarves with Rasheed at a large round table, set with silver on a white tablecloth.

The place was old-time elegant. Waiters in spotless jackets bowed as they poured water into silver cups. I ordered roast chicken. And oh my God, the *tension*.

Dani wouldn't look at me. I just wanted to sit and watch her, but I couldn't. I made myself not even (hardly) sneak a glance. Rasheed wouldn't look at me either. He was fidgeting with a bread knife, staring at it with burning eyes.

"I don't *understand* why you have to talk this way," Mrs. Shaheen said.

Rashi sighed. "The world is sick," he said patiently, like he was tired of explaining. "Anyone can see we've gone the wrong way—good people everywhere are shoved down and humiliated. The only cure is pure faith and rightful action. Those who choose wrong paths…" He looked at his parents. "The time comes when they will know."

"What will they know?"

"The flame. The fire of truth."

"God has given you a fine brain," his mom said. "This is how you use it?"

"If you would only pray, you would know."

"Of course I pray," she said. "I also *think*."

Rashi shook his head, crossed his arms. Mrs. Shaheen turned to my dad. "Why must young people pretend they know everything?"

My dad smiled. "It's a confusing world," he said. "It's always been tempting to grab for simple answers."

Rashi looked away.

"So, Luke," Assad said. "Did you visit the shrine?"

"Yeah, that place is pretty nice. And the *music*." I figured that would irritate Rashi. "I kind of really got into it."

"We call those songs *qawwali*," Assad said. "They are love songs to our greatest saints. Rahman Baba is called the Nightingale of Peshawar, because his songs are so sweet."

"Music is pornography," Rasheed said.

"How would *you* know?" Dani asked sweetly. He went dark red.

"I really liked the drum they used," I told Assad. "It had skin on both ends?"

"Oh yes, the *dholak*."

"Yeah! That's what the guy called it. He showed me a little of how he plays it. I really..." I took a breath, glanced at my dad. "I kind of want to learn it," I said to Assad. "I mean, I have some time and all, while we're here, and the guy who showed me was really friendly. I think I could maybe ask him. Like, for lessons."

Assad nodded. "You will need a drum."

I nodded. "I guess." I'd been thinking I could ask my dad for one. Like for Christmas?

But Assad said, "I happen to have a dholak." Rashi's head snapped up.

I said, "You do?"

"I do. I gave it to Rasheed, at a time when I was hoping he would discover our musical tradition." He glanced at Rashi, who glared at his bread knife. "Recently he gave the drum back to me," Assad said.

"Music is sin," Rashi mumbled.

"Tomorrow morning," Assad said to me, "when I come to take you to our museum, I can bring the drum."

"*Whoa*. Really?" I glanced at my dad, who smiled.

"I think it will be fine," Assad said. He glanced at Rashi again, a little sadly this time.

Our food came on silver trays. The waiters bowed as they spooned it onto our plates. My chicken was brown and steaming, with mashed potatoes and gravy and hot biscuits. *(Hot biscuits!)*

We started to eat. Rashi sat staring off. Then he blurted, "It's *not* too late."

We stopped. Looked at him.

"When someone has strayed from the truth, even if they think they are good Muslims…they will suffer," he said. "But they don't *have* to."

His mother and father peered at him. For an electric millisecond, Dani glanced at me.

"What in the world are you talking about?" his mom asked Rashi.

"The time comes when things must be done," he said. "The faithful do the will of God—the fire of truth purifies. But there is no suffering for true believers."

"Where do you pick up this nonsense?" his mother asked.

"You know," Dani said to her. "You *know*."

"No suffering indeed," Mrs. Shaheen said to us all. "My goodness, do we *want* a world where anyone who disagrees is shouted down—even killed? Where good teachers are persecuted just for teaching?"

"They can teach, but only truth! The truth purifies," Rashi repeated.

"You can't grow out of this phase one second too soon for me," his mother said.

"You are just a fool," he shot back.

"*Rasheed Abdullah Shaheen!*"

I'd never seen Assad mad before. "You will apologize to your mother or this family will be leaving," he said to his son. "Right away." He turned to my dad. "I am very sorry, but some behavior I will not tolerate."

Rashi shrugged. His father stood, pushed back his chair.

"All right," he said. "I will settle the check, and we will go."

Rashi's eyes widened; he glanced at his watch. I knew what he knew—that he couldn't let this break up early. That could mean my dad and me getting back to the Royal too soon.

He sat up straight. "I was only trying to help. Sorry if it's not what people want to hear."

"Unacceptable," his father said. "Speak to your mother. Apologize sincerely or we go."

Rashi glanced around. But then he said, to his mom, "Sorry." He looked away.

His mom's eyes were soft. "I just wish you would get over this," she said. "I do know where you go, who you listen to. But *why?*" She looked at him pleadingly. "Why associate with such people? Why let yourself believe such dangerous things?"

Rashi shook his head. He mumbled something no one could hear, then looked at me—but I didn't look back. I swept my eyes past Dani to their mom, who gazed pleadingly at her son.

When we got back to the hotel, I hopped out of the rickshaw, then stood looking at the hotel. What would I find inside? Yusuf and the cop had both said nothing would happen…but I didn't know. I just didn't know.

In a few seconds, I would.

My dad was clueless, of course. He strode happily past me through the front door, and I followed him as normally as I could. Walked to the desk, got my room key.

The downstairs was quiet. No sign of Yusuf, even. I got a prickly feeling. What did this mean?

My dad was already climbing the stairs. I came up quickly behind him.

"Um…going back to work?"

We were standing in the hall now, outside our rooms. "Yep." He sighed, jingled his key. "Always back to work."

"Yeah."

"But hey. That's nice about the drum, huh?"

"Yeah." I needed to stall him, or something. "You think it's okay? I mean, to borrow it or whatever?"

He shrugged, and nodded. "You'll be making him happy. Assad always wants to help someone learn."

I glanced over his shoulder, at his closed door. I was kind of frozen.

"Um...Luke, I wanted to say something," my dad said. "I was watching Rasheed and his dad today—and I thought, that could have been us, you know? You and me. I mean, just totally not connecting."

"Huh."

"All that anger," he said, not quite looking at me.

"Um..."

"They can't even talk to each other. I mean, it's sad."

"Yeah."

Okay, I thought, *I'm ready. Open the door.*

He looked up at me. "You think we're past that? I mean, I know you were pretty mad at me...and I guess I deserved it. But...you think we can, you know, talk now?"

"Now?"

"I don't mean *right* now, just in general. Out at Takht—it seemed like you saw. Maybe I've been too wrapped up in this work, but...did you maybe see why?"

"Um...sure. Yeah. I did."

Open the DOOR.

"Assad told me to give you space," he said. "He said to trust you, and trust Yusuf—and I know he was right. So, I mean, are we okay, you and me?"

"Um..."

Reassure him. He won't open the door till you reassure him.

"It's okay," I said. "Really. We're good."

His face relaxed. "Right! Well, guess I'll, you know. Get back to it."

"Right."

I waited. He said, "Is Yusuf around?"

"I don't know."

I waited. Finally, he went over, put the key in. Turned it...and opened the door.

I saw papers. Over his shoulder—piles. On the desk, on the bed. Piles of papers, and everything.

He looked back. "Want to come in…or something?"

I laughed. "Where would I sit?"

"Oh, I could…"

"No, it's cool. See you at dinner, Dad."

I turned and bounced down the stairs.

Yusuf came out of the kitchen. "Hey," I said.

"How was luncheon?"

"Pretty tense. What happened here, anything?"

"Nothing. No people, no police."

"*No* police?"

"No. Very quiet."

"The inspector said they'd send plainclothes guys."

"Yes, but you can tell. They did not come."

"Outside?"

"Maybe."

"My dad's room looks the same."

"Yes."

"Thanks."

"For what? For nothing."

"No. It was something."

Yusuf shrugged. "You are my guest. And my friend."

"Yeah. Hey, after dinner can we go visit your friends? In the bazaar?"

"It is Friday—we should stay here tonight. Everything is quiet. No trouble."

"What do you think those guys'll do? Anything?"

Again he shrugged. "I think we must be careful. Stay here. Listen to Bobmarli."

I laughed. "When in doubt, apply Bob."

"Sorry?"

"I mean, yes. I'll get my Walkman. Can I have tea?"

•

A while later I had "No Woman, No Cry" in my ears, sitting there bored in the dining room, when someone sat down across the table. It was Rasheed.

I jabbed at the Walkman to stop it. He just sat there, looking at me.

"Hey," I said. He stared. I said, "What?"

"Someone said, 'Stay away from the Royal. The cops will be watching.'"

"Huh."

"So much trouble, so much preparation. Then…nothing."

"Good. You're lucky this didn't work, Rashi. You don't go betraying your father."

"You don't understand—this is *bad*. That was the only peaceful way."

"No," I said. "The peaceful way is for you and those guys to find something else to do. Leave the professors alone."

"You don't get it—something has to *happen*. There is a fatwa! I tried to make things work so nobody got hurt. I tried."

There was a lot I could have said. But I didn't.

He threw up his hands. "I don't know what they'll do. This is bad, Luke."

"Why not just forget about it? Who cares? It's a *book*."

"You don't understand—a book is not nothing. A book can be a very big thing."

He stood up. "Get out of the country. As a friend, I'm telling you—get out tonight. Tomorrow."

"I can't, it's not up to me. My dad's not done working with your dad."

"I'm *telling* you. Do not leave this hotel. Stay away from the shrine, stay away from the music. Stay away from my house."

He started to go.

"And stay away from my sister," he said.

14.

Fire Is Fire

SATURDAY MORNING, I WAS FEELING pretty ready to get out of the hotel. Assad came in for breakfast, the drum under his arm, then we were going to the museum.

The drum was kind of fat but not that big. It was about as long as my forearm, made of dark wood with cords that ran the length of it and tightly held the skin at each end. Assad showed me the little rings on the ropes, how you could draw them tighter to raise the tension and tune up the sound.

I hit the wide end and it went *fup*. Not magic.

Assad said, "You need a teacher! The drummer you met at the shrine—do you know his name?"

"His first name's Wasi," I said. "I...don't know how to find him, though."

"Oh, I do—we'll go to Dabgari Bazaar. In Peshawar we have a street for everything: flowers, pots and pans, even kitchen sinks. The instrument makers and sellers have their shops in Dabgari, and upstairs are the little studios and rooms where the musicians hang out and give lessons and practice. If you want to hire them for a wedding or a party, you go there. But first the museum, yes?"

"Sure."

Out front—I had put the drum in my room, and my dad was in his, working—we got into a rickshaw. "Professors who are trying to finish books can't afford proper taxis," Assad said with a grin as we blatted into the intersection, then took a left on the Grand Trunk Road. We rode on it for a little while.

"The museum is my special place!" he yelled over the roar of the engine and the traffic. "The British opened it around 1900, and stocked it with treasures of our valley. We are just coming now—see it there?"

Above a garden of green hedges and trees rose a building that looked partly like a storybook palace, partly like a red brick fort. "Come! Come in!" said Assad, paying the driver and bustling inside.

In there past a marble-floored entryway was a simple high hall, like the white inside of a church. No one else seemed to be here. Assad spread his arms wide, to show the place off—and it was amazing.

Buddhas were everywhere.

Tall Buddhas stood draped in toga robes, their ancient stone gray against the white walls. Set up high were round Buddha heads, wise-looking and shadowy. Buddhas sat cross-legged on pedestals, and inside glass cases were lots of smaller ones—Buddha heads, little Buddhas standing and sitting, and Buddhas on long flat stones carved into scenes from old stories.

"We are looking *straight* back at Gandhara," Assad whispered excitedly. And even though the hall wasn't huge, it really was impressive, in a silent-eyewitness kind of way. Upstairs loomed a balcony, looking empty between the pillars of the arches.

"Definitely a cool place," I said.

"I chair the board—I'm always raising money for the museum. It's such a lot of work! Especially these days. See the hallways that lead off? Down that side is our Hall of Tribes. The other way leads to the Muslim Gallery. We have historic, handmade Korans."

He looked up at the looming sculptures. "This has been my second home," he mused. "For my children, too."

"Um…really? Do they come here?"

"Not Rasheed any longer." He sighed. "As you can imagine, my son disapproves of our principal collection. But Danisha still appreciates it. In fact, when groups of schoolgirls come to visit, she often gives the tour. She is a natural teacher," he said proudly.

My brain was shifting into gear. "Does she still…do that?"

"Actually, she is giving a tour this afternoon. My wife did not want her leaving the house, but Danisha insisted. Since she has no school for the time being, this is her one educational outlet. We are being very careful, but I do think this is important."

"Oh, for sure. So, like, do you keep boys and girls separate? I mean when school groups come."

"Well, we don't schedule boys' and girls' tours at the same time, but anyone who wants to learn is welcome. Knowledge should be for everyone. Now, Luke—come upstairs! Let me show you our model of Takht-i-Bahi."

Up there was a model they'd made, inside glass, of the ruin as it must have looked in its heyday. Up the slope it rose, a stacked-up complex of stone plazas and pedestals, with a fancy pagoda in the middle and tiny stone rooms all around.

"Those little chambers were where the monks lived and meditated," Assad said. "Dozens of statues and images would have been set all around. After the British started excavating the site, they found over five hundred sculptures. Incredible!"

"Oh yeah. Definitely. So, um...do I have to leave soon? I mean if girls are coming?"

"Oh, don't worry, they won't arrive till after lunch. Now, there was something I wanted to tell you...Oh yes! We have three ancient pottery jars in our collection that were unearthed at another Buddhist ruin in the valley. We have dated them to about 50 A.D. Each of the jars has the same inscription carved into it: '*To the Community of the four quarters*.'"

He said, "Isn't that fantastic? The inscriptions may have been speaking of the community of Buddhists—but they might also, your father and I think, have been referring to the whole world as one community. That's possible, don't you think? And at such an early time in history!"

"Wow. Totally interesting. So, will you be sticking around here today? I mean later."

"No, no, your father has us heading out to another ruin. Always more photography." He checked his watch. "I have just enough time to take us to Dabgari Bazaar and inquire after your drummer, then I must bring you back to the hotel. Unless you'd like to come see the ruin?"

"Uh, thanks, but... I'm kind of excited to mess around with the drum."

"Of course, the dholak. But let me show you just a few more treasures!"

And he was bouncing down the stairs, me trailing behind. Thinking hard.

Dabgari Bazaar looked like a regular street, I mean regular for Peshawar. Hard-packed and uneven, it had the usual jumble of walkers, horse carts and little vehicles pushing slowly past the sad-looking guys who stood around trying to sell oranges, peanuts or bananas from the neat piles they'd made on simple carts.

Inside one tiny shop, open like the others to the street, I saw a dented-up trombone and a tuba. Another shop had those accordion-box things, and hanging alongside the opening to a third shop were drums like mine. A man in pajamas sat inside with his feet planted against an unfinished dholak, leaning way back as he pulled the ropes tight.

Some boys and a few men came up while Assad was asking our rickshaw driver to wait. One of the boys said to me, "Hello, what is your country?"

"America."

"*Am*'rica! Disco!" The kid hit a *Saturday Night Fever* pose, finger pointed high, like he was in a white suit instead of a dirty T-shirt.

"*No* disco," I said. "Rock and *roll*."

"Yes! Rock and roll *disco!*"

Now all the boys were dancing and hopping around. "You guys are nuts," I told them, laughing as Assad talked with the men. When they were finished, everyone wanted to shake my hand.

"You are welcome!" one man said. "Welcome to our street of music!"

A boy went running off, then came back with a serious-looking man in a heavy mustache who talked with Assad. He said "Wasil" and waved at an upstairs window. From somewhere I heard the plinking of that banjo-sounding thing, and a high singer's voice.

Then we were racketing off in the rickshaw, everyone waving at me, the boys still leaping around like lunatics.

"They are excited to see you!" Assad shouted. "You have made a hit."

"What'd that guy say?"

"He says Wasil will come to you later today, at the hotel. We have already negotiated his fee."

"Cool. Um…what time will that be?" The rickshaw made an ugly swerve; I jolted into Assad.

"This afternoon later. Don't worry, he will come. I will ask your father to leave the money at the desk. It's not very much—these musicians have to work hard for their living. Many new ones are here, Afghan refugees who are also seeking work. A lot of musicians are in Peshawar just now, so this guy will be happy, even for this little job."

I had my chicken sandwich at the hotel. The professors ate quickly, then hurried upstairs and came down with my dad's camera bag and folded-up tripod. After they were definitely gone—I waited a few minutes, to make sure—I told Yusuf I was going upstairs. For a nap.

"Don't bring tea or anything. I'll be sacked out."

"You will be…"

"You know, asleep. Totally. For a while."

He got that crinkled look. "You are okay?"

"Oh sure. I mean…I don't know. I might be coming down with something."

"Coming down?"

"You know. Like if I don't rest I might get sick."

He was worried. "Peshawar is too dirty. Everyone gets sick sometimes."

"Yeah? Well, I'll just head upstairs. Wouldn't want *you* to catch it."

In the room, I sat looking at the drum and holding it, making myself wait. Then I went down some stairs I'd spotted in the back. At the bottom I pushed open a narrow door and I was in an alley. It opened onto the street that led back into the Old City.

Parked on the street close to the crazy intersection was that scooter rickshaw with the pink Lincoln and the World Trade Center on the back. That guy was okay.

"As salaam aleikum," I said to him, coming up.

The young man grinned. He had a wispy mustache that he really shouldn't have tried for, not yet. "Wa aleikum as salaam! Where is your friend?"

"Working. Very busy. So... I need to go to the Peshawar Museum."

"No problem. Three rupees, okay?"

"Um... sure." I had some money in my pocket.

I started to climb in, but he said, "No, please—you must not take first price!"

"Huh?"

"Listen to me. If some guy, a driver like me or a shopkeeper in the bazaar, if he tells you a price, you must say, 'Oh no. Too much!' Then you give a smaller price. Not too small, but maybe you say..."

"Like one rupee?"

"Say it strong. One rupee *only!*"

"One rupee only!"

"Good! Now people know they cannot cheat you. Maybe I say, 'Okay. *Two* rupees. Now we go.' You see?"

"Yeah. One rupee only!"

"No, two rupees is good price. Okay? You can pay at the end."

"Right. Two rupees only!"

He laughed and gunned the lawn-mower engine as I wedged myself in the back.

As we lunged into the intersection, I saw that two guys across the street were standing there looking at me. Were they just staring, like people here did sometimes—or were they watching? They turned and kept looking as we clattered into traffic.

The driver leaned back and shouted, "What is your country?"

"USA."

"Ah, very good! USA is the best place, yes?"

"Well… it's a good place," I said, watching the Grand Trunk Road go by.

"Any time you need, I am outside the hotel," the driver called back. "I am there early in the morning, also late at night. Any time you need, okay?"

"Yeah, sure. Thanks."

I'd just walked into the museum's entryway—you didn't have to pay or anything—when I heard her musical voice. Up ahead in the main hall. Quickly, quietly, I ducked up the stairs.

The balcony overlooked the big hall on both sides; I could stand behind a pillar and peek down. She had on a yellow-and-blue-patterned headscarf, and her pajamas were as pale green as sea glass. The girls, clustered close together, wore a school uniform: blue pajama tops and bottoms, white headscarves. Two youngish women who must have been their teachers were with them, also in headscarves.

"It is thanks to our Peshawar Valley that we have this famous image that the whole world knows, of this great saint," Dani was saying as she stood before the girls among the Buddha statues. "In his teachings, he said, 'Hate is not overcome by hate; hate is overcome by love. This is an ancient law.'

"What do you think about that?" Dani asked the girls. "Doesn't it seem like we are surrounded more and more by hatred these days, by people who see enemies everywhere? But how can that *be* the answer? I mean, how can we ever—"

"Miss?" A girl asked, "The teachings of this saint—are they Islamic?"

"Well," Dani said, "the Buddha lived centuries before the Prophet Muhammad, peace be upon him. But I think his teachings are much like those of our Sufi saints, and they *are* Muslim. The Buddha said, 'Seek the truth within,' and the Sufis say the same.

"And you can do this," she said, sounding more urgent now. "You *can* do this."

There was lots of murmuring, a small commotion. I snuck a look as a teacher cleared her throat. "Perhaps we could visit the Muslim Gallery now?"

"Yes," Dani said. "Of course."

They passed beneath me, into the side hall.

If you wait, museum tours do end. I heard her say goodbye to the girls in the front hall. When they were gone I snuck partway down the stairs.

"I think it was Martin Luther King who said that," I said.

Her feet scuffled. "Hello?"

"Up here. On the stairs."

"*Luke?*"

"Yep. I'm pretty sure Martin Luther King said that, about love beating hate. He was an American civil rights guy. I did a report on him."

"I know who Dr. King was," she said. "I guess he didn't say that first. But Luke, what are you *doing* here?"

"Remember how your dad wanted to show me the museum?"

"Yes…"

"Well, this morning he did. And he said you'd be giving a tour. So I came back. I just…"

"Shh! Don't move. Stay there."

I heard her walk away. There were no other footsteps, just hers. Then she was back, whispering from somewhere close, near the bottom of the stairs.

"Go upstairs, down the aisle and turn right," she said. "You'll be in the lecture hall. It should be empty. If it is, go to the end—you'll see a door. That's the committee room, where my father's board meets. Turn the handle very carefully. If you don't hear anyone inside, open the door. That room *should* be empty, too.

"If you see or hear anyone, come back and walk along the balcony. Don't say anything, I will hear you—and then you must go. Quickly. But if there's no one, then wait in the committee room. In a few minutes, if no one comes out of the office or enters the museum, I will come."

"Got it."

"Please—go *quietly*."

The lecture hall had only empty chairs. The door at the far end was open. No one was in the small room it led into, just a table with some chairs. The room had windows. It was sunny outside. I sat down, and waited.

After maybe two minutes that felt like fifteen, she came in. Closed the door. She stood there, back against it, staring at me. I sat down. She stayed standing, the table between us.

"Does my father know you came back here?"

"Of course not. He and my dad are off photographing a ruin. You think I'm not careful?"

"I think you're crazy. If we get caught..."

"I know. I don't want to put you in danger...I only wanted to talk."

She smiled, a little. "Only?" Then she went to the window, and stood beside it peering out.

"We can talk for no more than a minute," she said. "This is too risky."

"Are they...what happened about the lady who got killed?"

"The headmistress? Nothing. There will be nothing."

"But don't they investigate? *Was* it a murder?"

"Oh yes. There was a small item in the newspaper, saying she was purportedly shot on her way home from school. They really said 'purportedly,' and they said there were no witnesses. So no, they won't investigate. She was a woman," Dani said, as if that explained it.

"Whoever did it—do you think they could be Rashi's friends?"

"No, local extremists did this. And they will do more."

"What are you going to do? Can you go back to school?"

She peeked out the window again. "There is no school. Not for now, at least. I've been thinking…But you must not mention this. To anyone."

"I won't. What've you been thinking?"

"Well…I can disappear."

"What? Where?"

"Out there. I can go into the refugee camps. Ask for *panah*."

"For what?"

"Panah. It means asylum, protection from enemies. If someone appeals for this, we must give it. The camps are full of Afghan Pashtuns, hundreds of thousands. I can disappear."

She swung back from the window. "I can find RAWA there—join Meena's work. Teach women and girls."

"What about your family?"

Her face flushed. "For my parents…I think it would be terrible. But it will be worse if I am killed."

I had another idea. "Come to America," I said.

She looked up. "What?"

"We'll be going home soon—you could come. We could work it out. You could stay in my mom's apartment. I'd move in with my dad. It'd be okay!"

And I'd get to see you. Nobody would think that was wrong.

"I don't know."

"It'd *work*," I said, "and no shame to your family, right? Everyone here wants to go to America. You'd go to school with me. Maybe you could go to my dad's college. I bet you could!"

She held up her hand. "Did you hear something?"

We both listened…but no footsteps. Only silence.

"Um…listen," I finally said. "Speaking of family stuff. There's something else you should know about."

Her face got a curious look. I liked just looking at her. She sat down across the table, and said, "What?"

So I told her. About everything, quick as I could: the plot, the fatwa. Rasheed and Amal pulling me in. What was supposed to happen, but didn't.

"Our fathers' work? They would have *burned* it?"

"I think so. That's what Rashi said."

"My brother. Did he really say a fatwa must be followed?"

"Oh yeah."

"See, this is how they warp things. A fatwa is meant to be a learned opinion—something you consider deeply, as you decide what to do. But *they* say it's a command. They don't want to think, just be given answers. How can my brother believe fire solves anything? Fire is *fire.*"

"Yeah, well, there's more. Last night Rashi came to our hotel. He said his guys heard that cops were watching the hotel, so now they're all mad at me."

Her eyes widened. "What did he say?"

"He said not to go anywhere. Not to leave the hotel."

She rolled her eyes. "So you came here."

"Yep. Took a rickshaw," I said, a little proudly. "Hey, I'm not letting those guys tell me what to do. But it's, um, possible I might have been spotted. When we left the hotel, a couple guys might have been watching."

There was a long pause. Her eyes flicked toward the window again.

"You were good with those girls," I said. "Do you think you got them thinking?"

"Maybe not—that's what is sad. When they're young their minds are still open, but if they never meet anyone who sees the world differently, this culture will close in on them. I can promise you, in their secret hearts every one of those girls wants to have *choices.* But they keep having those taken away."

"Their teachers hustled them right out of the Buddha zone."

"Did you see that? People are becoming so fearful of learning anything they're not *supposed* to know. The extremists only want boys to memorize the Koran—and for girls, nothing at all. The veil and four walls. But—you must get back to your hotel! How will you get back?"

"Rickshaw, no problem. How do you get home?"

"The same. I put on a chador, jump in a rickshaw, go home. Do you have money?"

"Sure. And I've got a music lesson later, at the hotel. This guy I met at the shrine is coming over, to teach me on Rashi's drum."

She smiled. "That's nice. I think you are brave."

"What, to play the drum?"

"No—to find a way we could meet. I thought I would never *see* you again."

Her eyes were full, but now she looked upset. "We need to go," she whispered.

"Okay—but Dani." I had never said her name out loud before. "Can we write? Something?"

"I don't know." She stared past me, at the door. "People have guns in Peshawar," she said, very quietly now. "These men you crossed, we're lucky they are foreigners. Pashtuns would take revenge."

She pushed her chair back, stood up. The table was between us. That, and everything.

"After I leave, wait five minutes," she said. "Then go down the stairs and out the door. You can find a ride quickly out front. And please, when you go—move quickly."

"I will."

"Luke…this one time, I am glad you were crazy. But promise me you will stay safe. Until you get home. *Promise* me."

I nodded, but…I couldn't seem to say anything. She opened the door a tiny bit, and glanced out. Then she slipped through, and quietly and softly closed the door.

15.

Butterfly

HERE'S HOW, THAT EVENING, I found myself sitting on the floor in a dim upstairs room in Dabgari Bazaar, wearing Pashtun pajamas with a little crowd of musicians and their friends:

When I got back from the museum, Wasil the drummer was waiting in the dining room of the Royal. I brought him upstairs. He was a nice guy with a friendly smile, and when he sat on the bed and played my dholak, its *thump thump POCK, thump thump POCK* rhythm was real and exciting again. But when I put my hands on the drum, all I got was *fup*.

Fup.

"You can get this." Wasi was nodding, smiling. "It takes a bit of work, sure. All music does. But if you get the two basic sounds, you can build from there. Find the voice of your drum! Then *speak* with it."

I liked him. He was trying. I had thought the drum would be easy, because it looked simple—but, okay. I watched, I listened. I tried. Promised I would practice. Then, after a while, there was a knock.

Yusuf had a tray with tea. I think he was making sure everything was okay. When he left, Wasi and I sat drinking tea and talking about music. From the pocket of his vest, he brought out a cassette. *Saturday Night Fever.* White suit on the cover, finger pointing high.

"This is the only Western music I have," Wasi said. "It is good, yes?"

"It's good for disco, but…hang on a second."

I opened the drawer and lifted out the red cassette case, the Walkman and the headphones. When I zipped the case open, Wasi's eyes got wide.

"This is Bruce Springsteen. He *rocks,*" I said, pulling that one out. "And you should hear the Police for sure. But first…"

I slipped in *Catch a Fire,* and handed him the 'phones. He put them on, and I hit Play.

At dinner, Yusuf got alarmed when I told him Wasi had invited me to come tonight to the music street, and to bring my cassettes. As the professors talked about their project, Yusuf stood behind them, frowning and shaking his head at me. He backed up into the shadows by the kitchen door, and waved at me to come over.

I went.

"That boy warned you not to leave the hotel," Yusuf whispered. "You told me this."

"But I got invited to hang out with musicians, man! Think about it. It's dark out, we take a rickshaw, the traffic swallows us up. No worries. Anyway, why should I care what Rashi said? Him and his friends are losers."

"Maybe, maybe not. But we must be smart."

"Okay, sure. Smart. You got any ideas how?"

He was thinking. Then he said, "Maybe I do."

That's why, when we left my room a little later with the typewriter *clack-clacking* next door, Yusuf was wearing jeans and a T-shirt, like he did sometimes when he was off work, but I had on his rolled-edges cap, his brown vest, and a long-tailed, tan pair of his shalwar kameez.

"I feel ridiculous," I said as we came down the stairs.

"To look like a Pashtun, this is ridiculous?"

"It's not that—it just isn't me. Those guys'll laugh at me."

"No. You are showing respect. You like our music, you appreciate our culture."

"Yeah, but…"

His face was set. "If we go to Dabgari Bazaar, we go like this. Or we don't go."

"We're going." I had my cassettes, Walkman and drum in my backpack. "I got *invited*."

"You may as well look like a Pashtun," Yusuf said with a shrug. "You are just as stubborn."

When we got to the music bazaar, Yusuf stayed downstairs, looking up and down the street as Wasi brought me up some narrow stairs to this second-floor room. It was lit by a single yellowish bulb. One wall had newspaper pages stuck up on it, like super-cheap wallpaper; another had two beat-up dholaks hanging from nails. Four or five guys who'd been sitting on the floor all stood up, and Wasi introduced me all around.

Everyone was smiling and nodding as we shook hands. One guy had that violin-like instrument, which Wasi said was a *rabab*. Up close, it had tuning keys along the side and at the end of the neck; the guy plucked it like a guitar, but the body had a tight-stretched skin that gave it the deep-banjo sound. Someone else had that box accordion, which they said was a harmonium. Now the man with the thing like a clarinet ducked into the room. I asked him, "What *is* that?"

"It is a clarinet!"

"Oh. Right."

"I have said you wish to learn the dholak," Wasi said. "They want to make music with you."

"But all I can do is make a *fup*."

When this was translated, everyone laughed, and discussed this. Much discussion, with gestures at me. Smiling. Waving at my clothes. Discussing.

"What are they saying?"

"That you are an American and you appreciate our culture. They think this is very good," Wasi said. "And it's okay, you don't have to play the drum." He reached behind him, brought out a tambourine. It was a regular tambourine, with a skin, a wooden hoop and jingles.

"How about this?"

"Oh! Well…"

"Don't worry, I will help you. Just strike it here, against the bottom of your hand, when I show you. All right?"

"Okay."

The guys agreed: Tambourine is good! Very good! *Much* encouragement. So the harmonium guy got a drone going, one long wheezy note; then the rabab guy picked out something slow and sharp. He played that and played it, going faster as Wasi came in with the dholak, the harmonium wheezing up and down like we were floating on it. The drum and rabat synced up, and that was nice:

Dum pockATa, POCKa, POCKa,
dum pockATa, POCKa POCKa

Wasi was looking at me and nodding on what, as I listened, I could hear was the first beat on his drum:

Dum *pockATa,* **POCK**a, POCKa,
dum *pockATa,* **POCK**a POCKa

I tried to hit that first beat on my tambourine but missed it. He kept nodding, on that beat…and then I had it. I had it, then lost it—but he nodded, still on it…and then I had it.

I *had* it. And the music was good. I can't say I understood it, the guys kind of repeated the same bit of a tune over and over—but they also changed it, jammed on it, the clarinet in there too. And the rhythm was right there—when I'd lose it I'd look at Wasi and he'd nod again, right in the spot.

Dum *pockATa,* **POCK**a, POCKa,
dum *pockATa,* **POCK**a POCKa

And I was part of it! As they swelled and repeated and jammed, I kept that one simple beat. Then it was like I stopped thinking; my sound was just part of it. A player smiled at me as we played and I *was* part of it, it was music and we were making it.

This was an incredible few minutes of my life. We were in that yellow-lit room halfway around the world with newspaper on the wall and the rhythm inside different music, and we were ringing the music off everything. Ringing it together. It was *great*.

When it was over—I don't know how long we played, I kind of lost track—but when it finally ended, everyone was happy. They clapped me on the back. Shook my hand.

"You have played well!" Wasi said.

"Thanks, man. You kept me in there."

"Only a little. You found the beat. With all drumming, you must keep that first beat. If you know where that is, you can't get lost. This is a good lesson for you, okay?"

He stuck out his hand. We shook. "Now," he said, "I have told these guys about *your* music." He said something in Pashto, and one of the guys who'd been squeezed against the wall, listening, brought out a cassette player, the cheap kind shaped like a flat shoebox. He set it in front of Wasi.

"Okay," I said, and fished the red case out of the backpack. Much discussion of this, and even more as I zipped it open and the guys saw the twelve cassettes. *Much* discussion. Fingers pointing. Excitement!

"What should I play?"

"It is your choice," Wasi said. "Any music, we like to hear."

I'd been thinking about this. I'd considered Bruce: *Born in the USA*? But then I thought: *You know what to play. You know.*

So I slipped in Bob's *Natty Dread*. I'd set it up earlier: side one, song two. "No Woman, No Cry."

They swayed as they listened, then Wasi was *pock*eting along. "See?" he said to me. "Downbeat, *up*beat. Downbeat, *up*beat." I heard it, and then the clarinet was improvising along, very pretty, everyone listening closely. And when the song was done and I'd switched it off, they started *playing* it.

Not exactly the same, but Wasi had the reggae feel already in the rhythm—and the harmonium did its droning, and the rabat guy was pretty closely picking out the melody. They were messing with it, changing it, making it more like something of theirs. The jam didn't last long, but it was very cool.

"Play another!"

So I started "Born in the USA." This didn't catch on so well. I wanted them to love it, but the big rock sound didn't come through the little speaker. When Bruce sang "Born in the USA," they understood that, and liked it—grinning, they pointed to me: "USA!" But when Bruce got to the part—I hadn't thought about this—when he's sent to kill the yellow man, Wasi got a puzzled look.

The song didn't sound right anyway. No bass at all. I switched it off.

"Okay," he said. "Very nice."

"It's usually played really loud. It doesn't sound right on this."

"Yes."

The clarinet guy clapped me on the back. He said, "USA!"

It was still early evening when the rickshaw brought me and Yusuf to Karim Pura Bazaar. Nasim's shop was open. I was so amped up about the music, no way did I want to go right home. Yusuf wasn't thrilled, but he was okay with us coming here. I think he felt safer with his friends.

The tea-making place was open. So were more shops, each one a narrow lighted opening in the nighttime murk. No streetlights in this old, old neighborhood.

"Hello, my friends!" Nasim said, and he called for tea. As word got around that we were there, some other guys came. I never knew how word flashed around Peshawar so fast.

Imtiaz showed up; he said hello but then sat silently. I couldn't tell if he was mad at me, for not somehow sending him to America. He just didn't say anything.

This time the friend with the round face, who hadn't spoken the first night, told me his story. He had tried to sneak over borders into

Germany for work, avoiding the regular crossings because he had no visa. Just below his goal, he got caught in Austria; he was given a ticket to Iran and put on a train. Halfway there, he jumped off. Two months later, with twenty-four other Pakistani boys, he made it back to the Austrian border, where they all got caught by the army there.

The third time he tried, he made it to Vienna. Got caught there. Sat in jail for two months, then was flown back to Pakistan.

"I'm in the airport in Karachi, with two other Pakistani guys," he said. "They tell us to sit. They have my passport, ID card. I say to them, 'I go to the toilet.' Then I sneak out and take a taxi. I come back here."

He sat quietly. Then: "I will try again."

"Hah! Really?"

"Yes." Again, he sat thinking. "You can go to Germany, yes? No problem?"

"I think so. Pretty much."

"Yes." He spoke with the other guys, in Pashto. They said something about passports. The round-faced guy shook his head.

"A Pakistani passport has no value," he said. "U.S., British, German—if we can get these, they have value. But ours has none."

"I didn't know that."

"It is true."

In the lane, a beggar trudged up. He had no chin, couldn't close his mouth. Yusuf gave him a coin, and he trudged on.

As we sat, quiet and thoughtful now, I watched a man who sold vegetables across the lane. He sat cross-legged on a ledge, a foot or so above the street; he had a military buzz cut and wore an old soldier's sweater. He had just shaped up his little manger of leafy greens, celeries and radishes when a motor scooter blatted by and gave him a shot of black exhaust, right in the face.

The guy grimaced and waved the smoke away from his stuff, which I figured he needed to sell to feed his family. For a second, I wondered how it was to be that guy.

The boys in the shop were laughing about another story. When they settled down I said, "Yusuf? How big is your family?"

The other boys fell quiet.

"My family?"

"Well...yeah. You said your dad works at the hotel, right?"

"Yes. He cooks."

"And your mom? Is she around?"

"No." He said no more.

"Do you have brothers? Sisters?"

"I have...a sister," Yusuf said. He wasn't looking at me. Nobody was looking at me. Or at him.

"Oh." I didn't know how to ask more. Or if I should.

Then Nasim said, "Tell him."

Yusuf didn't respond.

"He is your friend," Nasim said. "You should tell him."

Yusuf gazed at me, thoughtfully, for a time. Then he said, "My family lived in Kabul. My sister was little, only five. After the Russians came, there was a lot of trouble. Many men, thousands of men, were taken to prison. Most never came out. My father had worked for an American family, diplomats, as a cook. So when the Communists took over and the family left, he got word that he was in danger of being arrested.

"We just left. In the middle of the night, we took three suitcases, for my father, my mother and me to carry. A friend of my father's who had a taxi drove us outside Kabul. We walked all the rest of that night, and all the next day, and the next and the next. We walked for more than a week."

"What did you eat? Where did you sleep?"

"What we could. Where we could. To Afghans a traveler is a guest, the same as here. Sometimes it was dangerous for people to help us, but every time someone could, they did. We only had to sleep outdoors for two nights.

"The second night that we had to do that, we were too tired.

We slept by the road, and in the morning we were hungry. We wanted to make a small fire so we could make tea, cook a little bread. We were looking along the roadside for sticks, dried grass, anything to burn. There was a farm field. It was abandoned because of the fighting, so it was full of sticks. You know, old crops. My sister, she didn't know not to walk into a field."

"Why not walk in a field?"

"Mines. The Russians have put thousands of mines in the fields, in the villages—every place they cannot control. You have to stay right on the road."

"Couldn't there be mines in the roads?"

He shrugged. "The Russians use the roads too, so mostly they mine the places where only Afghans go. Fields, villages, hillsides.

"There is a kind of mine called a butterfly. They're dropped from helicopters, and they have little wings, so they float down spinning," Yusuf said. "They are green and small, made of plastic. The plastic is soft, and if you squeeze it the mine explodes. A lot of kids see them and think they are something to play with.

"When my mother looked around for my sister, she saw she was in a field, and was bending to pick up something. My mother screamed but my sister didn't know what was wrong. My mother ran. She got there and reached for it just as my sister started to play with the thing."

The guys in the shop said nothing. I finally said, "What happened?"

Yusuf's mouth was tight. "My mother covered most of my sister with her body. But my sister's hands were torn to pieces."

A cold shudder went through me. "What about your mom?"

"It was a small mine, but she was cut up terribly, by the…the metal. The bits."

"Shrapnel," I said. "Pieces of the mine."

"Shrapnel. Yes." Yusuf said it again slowly. "Shrap…nel."

"What happened then?"

He shrugged. "It was wartime in the countryside. No hospitals, no doctors. We cleaned their wounds the best we could—we tore up clothing from our suitcases and made bandages, then my father and I put them on our backs. We left everything behind. My father carried my mother, I carried my sister. It was very hard, they were in too much pain. Their bandages were soaked in blood, then so were we. We were sure they would die.

"A freight truck stopped for us. They gave us water, and my father gave them money. We rode to the border, through the pass, in the back underneath sacks of grain. It was very dirty. My mother's wounds got infected. We got them to Peshawar. At a hospital here, they took my sister's hands."

"They took her *hands*?"

"Yes. Cut off." Yusuf drew the blade of one hand across his other wrist. "They said otherwise, she would die."

"What…what about your mom?"

"The infection was too bad. In the hospital, she died."

"Well…God, Yusuf. How's your sister? What can she do?"

"She cannot do. She only sits. My father does the cooking, the cleaning, everything. I help—I work, bring home a little money, do some cleaning, wash the dishes. We feed my sister. Most men will never do these things. My sister, she sits. She is broken. I think she will never fix."

"Can't she get, like, artificial hands? Or something?"

He shrugged. "We are refugees."

"What's her name? Your sister."

"Meena. It means 'light.'"

Same as Dani's hero. I shivered. No clue what to say.

Yusuf looked down into his tea. Then back up.

"Maybe I don't see these things the same as all Pashtun men," he said. "Some say what my father and I do at home is women's work, that we should never do it. But if we don't, who does? We can't afford to pay someone, so who?"

"Women are for cooking the meat, not to meet!" said a man in the street who'd stopped at the counter, to listen. Nasim said something sharp to him. The man shrugged. Moved on.

Quiet. We were quiet.

"Do you think it's wrong, the way women are treated here?" I asked. I was a little scared the guys might get angry, but they didn't. They waited for Yusuf to answer, and listened when he did.

"I do think this is something that must change," he said. "When I clean the dishes, after I finish I look at my hands. They don't become women's hands. They are just hands."

Again, I looked at the others. They were quiet. Nasim nodded. That was all.

"I'm sorry," I said.

"Okay."

They were all thoughtful. After a bit, Imtiaz spoke.

"You know the word for 'mother' always has 'M,'" he said.

"Huh?"

"I like to study language," he said. "In our languages, all the words for 'mother' have 'M.' In Pashto we say Mor, and in Urdu, the main Pakistani language, they say *Ammi*. In Hindi, the biggest language in India, they say *Maji*. In Punjabi it's *Mai*, and in Farsi, the language of Iran, they say *Maadar*."

"In German they say *Mutter*," I said.

"In French it is *Mère*," said Nasim.

"How do you know this?" Imtiaz asked.

"I know this," Nasim said. "I would like to go to France."

"See?" Imtiaz said. "They all have 'M'."

"I guess they do," I said.

"It is not the same with 'father.'"

"No?"

"No. It is not the same."

The guys fell quiet again. I found myself watching the teashop boys as they ran in and out of the place across the lane, bringing cups and trays all around the bazaar.

"That never changes much, does it? The teashop."

"No," said Nasim. "And next to it, see the bakery? That's where they make the *naan*."

"What's a naan?"

"It is our bread, flat bread. Everyone eats it. Just watch."

So I did. The bakery had a wood platform on which the baker sat cross-legged; the brick oven below him had a little metal door at street level, and when they opened that to stoke the fire I could see bright orange flames in there.

The baker seemed like a cheerful character. His two young sons mixed and moistened the dough, shaped it into lumps and worked those into flat ovals. With a long-handled wood paddle, the father picked up each oval and dipped it downward through an opening on his platform, patting it onto the oven's inner wall. Then he'd stick a long metal pick with a hooked end into the oven and pull up a new-baked naan, spinning on the hook. Another son would wrap the steaming flatbread in newspaper and put it out for sale. Every naan went out hot.

Nasim called across the lane, and a boy brought one. Nasim unwrapped the brown-edged bread, and held it out. "With your fingers, just tear off some," he told me.

It was beautiful to eat, the naan—crusty outside and inside moist and delicious, soft and warm. As we passed it and shared it around, I felt pretty sure it had been just this way, that people had been eating this bread just this way since the time of Gandhara, the time of Jesus Christ, the time when Karim Pura Bazaar was young.

The evening got later as the guys chatted, told stories, laughed. They tried hard to talk in English, but kept slipping into Pashto. I didn't mind. Nasim had a radio going, and as Pakistani pop warbled in the background, I watched the traffic trudge past and remembered how it felt to *play* with those guys. How they'd picked right up on "No Woman, No Cry."

I was thinking about the lyrics of that song, how they tell about sitting with your friends in this same kind of place—in a poor city neighborhood, watching people go by and talking and sharing food. I got more and more excited; I really got the song now! I'd been part of the music and now I was part of this. I kept thinking about that, and the song kept playing in my head.

At last the other guys drifted off. The bazaar was shutting down. Yusuf and I said goodbye to Nasim, who shook hands and said to come back tomorrow as he got ready to draw down the metal grate and padlock his shop.

The lane back to the hotel was dark. I got my Walkman out of the backpack, slipped in *Natty Dread,* put on my phones, and rewound till I found the start of "No Woman, No Cry."

"Listen, okay?" I said to Yusuf. "We were playing this, back at the music street. And the words—it's like they're about tonight! About hanging out back there."

I started to slip the headphones on him so he could hear it, but Yusuf shook his head. "Not here. After we get back."

"No, but just for a second. I think this is really cool—I get what Bob *meant* now. Just listen, okay?"

So Yusuf accepted the 'phones, and I turned the song up in his ears. I had the drum out now, and I was making my *fup* to the sound leaking through the headphones, shuffling around with my drum in the dark, and neither of us heard footsteps coming from a pitch-dark alley just after we'd passed it.

It was all dark and nobody could see much—but Yusuf had the 'phones on, he had the T-shirt and jeans on so he looked like the American, and they hit him in the head and threw something over him, like a sack. As his knees buckled from the blow, they wrapped him up, pulled him off his feet, and I was shoved hard. My knee banged on the ground and my shoulder slammed into the corner of a building. I dropped the drum with a *bonk,* and someone grabbed it. I heard a ripping sound, then another *bonk*; and dark figures hauled my friend back into the alley.

A rickshaw's motor started; its headlight blasted the wall beside me. The vehicle lurched out from the alley, swayed onto the uneven lane and shot off in the other direction. Footsteps ran away up the street.

My shoulder hurt and my knee was scraped up bad. In a stunned daze I fumbled in the gritty murk for things on the ground. Found the Walkman, the headphones still attached. They must have knocked those off him. I sat on my butt and felt all around until I found the drum. But something was wrong with it.

The ropes were loose. At one end I felt torn skin. So that was the ripping sound—they'd slashed it.

I sat on the street. I held the ripped drum and listened, for something. A police siren? But it was dark, there was nothing. It was quiet. And I was alone.

16.

Dawn

GETTING BACK TO MY ROOM was a nightmare. In the cave-like shops on the butcher street they were chopping up skinned animals, piling up carcasses lit red and raw by flickering lamps. I stumbled on, into darkness again.

My shoulder ached bad. Yusuf's pajama pants were ripped at one knee, rawness behind the torn cloth. Limping and holding my hurt arm against my side with the dark buildings leaning over me, I came to one that had colored lights strung up and down. I heard music from inside. A drum. A bit of light showed around the closed door.

A boy came up. "It is a wedding."

"Uh?"

"Yes. Wedding tomorrow." He looked at me. "You are okay?"

I just mumbled, and stumbled on.

The busted drum bumped against my leg. My back was wet with sweat under the backpack, my head was foggy and I was in a dark tunnel, groping for the place where I could be safe.

At the hotel, the guy at the front desk glanced up but I got past him as fast as I could. I didn't want to be seen, didn't want to get in trouble, just wanted to lock my door and be safe. I should have pounded on my dad's door and told him what happened; but I opened my own door instead, quiet as I could.

Lie down. Lie down.

I did. I was cold. I did not cry. If I never made a sound, if I pulled the blanket up high, then everything and everyone would leave me alone. Leave me alone. And I could sleep.

I woke up; it was still dark. My shoulder hurt and the pulsing in my knee said it needed to be cleaned. I got up and groped my way to a bathroom in the back of our floor.

I pulled up the left pants leg with the red-stained rip. The knee had only bled a little. I got some water in my cupped hand and rinsed it, the water splashing and getting the pants wet. I rubbed some soap into the scrape, and rinsed. I'd had worse. I hurried back to my room and stripped off the clothes. My shoulder was sore, but it seemed to work okay.

I sat on the bed. My head was clearer now. Through the window was a vague fuzziness. The first light of dawn would come soon.

I pulled on my jeans and my black Bob Marley T-shirt. Put on my jacket. The shoulder hurt when I raised my arms. But I knew what I had to do.

What do I need?

Nothing. Well, money. Into the jeans pocket I stuffed what rupee notes I had—a twenty, three tens and some fives and ones.

Okay, a note.

Yeah...it was only fair. I found the little blue spiral notebook that my dad had said I had to bring on this trip, in case I might learn something. I ripped out a page.

If I don't come back, I wrote, *ask Rashi where I am.*

I left the note on the desk. Closed my door quietly, then slipped down the back stairs.

The traffic circle was almost empty. From a cart with a metal tank on it, a man sprayed water on the intersection. Two women in burqas were stooping to sweep the wetted-down surface, using brooms with no handles. They stepped back when a painted-up truck went by. Then they bent to work again.

Shivering in the chill, I looked up and down the intersection, and both ways out along the Grand Trunk Road. I was hungry and thirsty and sore—but mainly I was hoping.

Will he come? And if he does come, will he know? Will he remember the way?

Out of the murk emerged a little rickshaw. I couldn't tell, I thought maybe...but I couldn't tell. It came through the intersection, then swung onto the side street and pulled right up, and I saw the pink Lincoln and the twin towers. As I walked up to it, the driver said, "Hello, good morning!"

"Hey. Listen," I said as I wedged myself onto the bench in back. "Do you remember taking me to a house in University Town? It was me and my friend."

He thought a second. "I remember it."

"Can you take me there again?"

"Yes." He studied me. "It is very early. You are okay?"

"Um...yeah."

"You would like some tea? Just wait—I will get tea."

"No, man, thanks. I just really need to get to that house."

"Okay. Last time your friend paid three rupees. It's good price, Pashtun price. Okay?"

"How about five rupees and you go fast?"

"Okay!"

He gunned it and we almost slid sideways, racing across the wetted-down circle.

As I paid the driver, the chokidar with the bow-tied beard came out of his hut. It wasn't quite dawn. He smiled, we shook hands. He opened the gate and let me through.

I creaked open the front door, and there in the dim hall was Rashi with his mouth open. A canvas bag hung from his hand.

I flicked my head back toward the porch. He came out with me, and set the bag down. Closed the door softly.

"Your friends are *idiots*," I said.

"Shhh," he whispered. "Everyone is asleep."

"And you wouldn't want them to find out," I whispered back, "would you? Everything you've done. You wouldn't want them to know."

He blinked. Then he squared his shoulders.

"I was about to phone for a taxi," he said softly. "I am leaving this place."

"Yeah? To go where?"

"Into training. For jihad."

"You're taking off pretty early, Rashi."

"This is what soldiers do."

"Oh yeah, you're a *big* warrior. Where is he?"

"Who?"

"My friend. Your friends took him, as if you didn't know. They thought he was me, because it was dark and they're idiots. Throw a bag over a kid in the dark. So *brave*."

"I don't know what you're talking about."

"I don't believe you, Rashi, but you know what? *I don't care.* Go play soldier if you need to—but first you're going to do something. You're going to go back in and make a phone call."

His eyes shifted. "We don't have a telephone."

"You just said you were calling for a taxi. So go call your friends."

"What? Why?"

"Tell them if they want me, they can have me."

His eyes bulged. "What?"

"You heard me—but on one condition. They let my friend go."

"Luke, these people—just leave this alone. I told you, get out of Peshawar. I *told* you."

"Anyone else awake in the house?"

"Not yet. But soon."

"So tiptoe back in really sneaky, like you were about to sneak out. Tell your friends to bring Yusuf here. Tell them I'll be watching—tell them Yusuf has to be unhurt. As soon as I see them let him go, as soon as I see he's okay and free, I walk out. If they've hurt him, the deal's off—but if he's okay, they let him go and they get me."

He shook his head at me. "Luke—no."

"Yes. Do it."

"*Why?*"

"Because I've realized something, Rashi. My friend's family needs him, I happen to know how much—but to your guys, he's no use. No leverage. But an American? *That's* leverage. I'm the one they wanted. So that's the deal."

"Are you crazy? You can't *do* this."

"But I can, Rashi. And what can your guys do to me? Hurt me and they'll be *screwed*. Even they'll know that."

"Luke…Luke. We can go to the cafe, we can talk. Okay? I've got my—"

I held up my hand. "Tell them if they bring my friend here and drop him off, unhurt so I can see, they get me. Period."

"Why should I do this?"

"Because if you don't, I tell your dad what you tried to do to him. And I tell the police you were part of a kidnapping. You can't play soldier from a jail cell, Rashi."

He stood staring at me. Then he shrugged, and whispered, "Okay, if this is what you want. But let me tell you something—*you will remember my name.*"

"What? I already—"

"You think you can mock my faith, make me look like a fool the way *they* do in there." He jabbed his thumb back toward the house. "Everyone thinks they're so much smarter than me, so much better than me. But soon, *everyone* will hear my voice."

"Rashi…"

"When justice comes, your face will be in the dirt—and you'll cover your head in shame because you could have been with us. You *could* have been. But you will be nothing, and *our* word will be law.

Justice is coming, Luke—you'll know it when it comes. God's justice is coming for *everyone*."

He turned around, opened the door and slipped inside to make the call.

I stuck my head in the chokidar's little hut. In here he had a rope bed and a camp stove, a dented aluminum pot on it steaming. He smiled.

"Good morning, sir," he said. "Will you take tea?"

"Um...sure. Thank you. So, you speak English?"

He stood up straight. "Muhammad Shah Ishaq, lance corporal, British Indian Army. North Africa campaign. Twice wounded, Libya and Egypt. Honorably discharged."

He glanced at the wall. Stuck there by a tack, the only thing on the wall, was a soldier's medal.

"Corporal," I said, "I need your help."

He nodded. Saluted. And gave me tea.

I was hoping it wouldn't take long—I remembered that the house of Rashi's friends, Sheikh Osama's group, was somewhere nearby. I was a little shaky, but as I waited, with Muhammad Ishaq standing by his door keeping lookout, I was focused. On being ready.

I heard a car come up the street.

Muhammad Ishaq turned, and nodded. Through the door I saw the white Toyota, the one I'd seen Osama riding in, pull up and stop. Two guys were in the front seat, three in the back. The one crammed in the middle in back had on a dark blindfold.

For a long moment, nothing happened. Then there was movement in the car. The back door on its far side opened. One guy got out, then he yanked Yusuf out so hard that my friend stumbled and fell on the street.

Yusuf got up, pulling off the blindfold. He looked around once—then he hurried up the street, turned a corner quickly, and was gone.

I stepped through the door of the hut. The morning light was really bright. I stood there, blinking in the sun.

PART THREE

17.
Superstars

THE BLINDFOLD WAS TIGHT. The rope around my wrists was tight; I could only raise my hands a little. Beneath my legs I could feel the woven rope and rounded-wood frame of the bed. If there was any light in the room, I couldn't see it. I did not know where I was.

What did you DO?

The fear was like a waterfall, roaring in silence inside. Everything had changed so fast. I'd been totally focused on setting Yusuf free—and somehow I'd felt sure they wouldn't do anything to me. They couldn't. I mean, come on.

But that was before they'd blindfolded me in the back seat of the car, tied my hands, and never said one word the whole ride until finally the car stopped and they yanked me out, then pushed me—no words at all, just *push, push* in the back, not hard enough to make me fall but steady and insistent, showing they were in charge—up some steps to an upper floor.

They pushed me down so I was sitting on this bed. They tied some more rope—it squeaked a little when they tied it—between what was already around my wrists and the bed. Tied it to the leg of the bed, I guessed. Then they left.

They just left.

From the other side of the door after they'd closed it, I heard muttered voices in another language. Then nothing. Traffic sounds outside. Nothing else. Inside, the silent waterfall started to roar.

I'd never been tied up helpless before—and no joke it was terrifying. You *need* freedom, the way you need air right after you've been punched in the stomach. But when you've had the wind knocked out, after a second or two of panicky struggle you're breathing again, you're okay; but nothing I did here made any difference. No matter how bad I freaked out inside, I couldn't get freedom. I couldn't get *anything*.

What did you DO?

I had not said a word to them. Just like they hadn't spoken to me, I hadn't asked them where we were going or what they were going to do—nothing. I felt proud of that. I knew they wanted me to be scared. I knew they wanted me to cry or beg, but I had not done or said anything to show them how shaken-up I really was—and now I could feel the anger rising in my chest, mixing with the quiet-roaring fear. These guys were wannabes and losers, I would *not* give in to them—but what was going to happen? I was thirsty and hungry and what about when I had to pee? What if they just *left* me here?

I pulled hard with my arms. I yanked my tight-bound hands back and forth, but that only hurt. Nothing gave way, nothing loosened up. *Ohmygod please please let me GO!*

Stop.

Breathe.

My breath was coming in panting gasps, hiccups almost. I focused on smoothing it out, settling a little. *Just...breathe.* As I did, the twitching and trembling settled down. So did the circling and popping of panicky thoughts and fears...and I was okay. I could settle myself. I could.

Okay.

Something else I could do was listen. If I listened, I could hear sounds.

And if I stayed steady, if I kept on breathing steady, I could think.

Traffic. I could hear traffic sounds. They were muffled by walls and closed windows, but yes: there was the rattle of a rickshaw, the rumble of a truck or bus. And horns—honking horns. I'd got so used to hearing them, in Peshawar, but I stopped and thought about what it meant that I could hear them now.

The headquarters, or whatever they called it, of Rasheed and Osama's group—the Services Bureau, that was it—was in University Town. So was the Shaheens' house. That was a quiet kind of suburb. You didn't hear much traffic noise there.

So I was somewhere in the city.

For once in Peshawar, I felt grateful for the noise. People were out there. Not far away.

I'd been so worried about Yusuf—in the dark last night, it sounded like they hit him really hard. But this morning when they let him loose, he looked okay. Maybe a little confused, but they'd just shoved him blindfolded out of the car. They told him to run. And he did.

They let him loose. So they could do the same for me. But what would they want? To show everyone here what they did to people who crossed them? Show the world how crazy they were?

How crazy *were* they?

The panicky terror was roaring again, and now I was losing it—shaking, twisting, yanking against my ropes but that *hurt.* Stop.

Stop.

Try to breathe. You have to breathe. Nothing else you can do.

What did I DO?

Nobody came to ask if I had to use the toilet, or if I needed a drink or some food or anything. The inside of my mouth was dry and crackly as paper. It hurt. I could feel the weave of the bed on my butt. Decided to see if I could lie down.

Slow and careful, I did it. Now I was on my side, bound wrists up by my face. Okay. I didn't know if I could get back up, but it was a little better, lying down. Maybe I could sleep or something.

And maybe I did. When everything is dark, it's hard to tell if you've been asleep or not... but I heard the door open. And it closed.

Someone was in the room.

"Sit up," said a hard voice.

I struggled, pushed with my hands... and then I was sitting again.

Fingers touched my blindfold, and they rolled up the bottom of it just a little. Now I could see, but straight down only: my jeans and the edge of the bed, rope wrapped around the wood—and pressed khaki pants and a pair of Adidas Superstars. White leather, black stripes. Clean and bright as new.

"Do you need to relieve yourself?" the hard voice asked. I shook my head. The voice barked something in another language, and the door opened again. Steps came close, and a plastic tray was set beside me on the bed. On it was a cup of tea, milky brown, and an oval naan speckled brown from the oven.

"You may eat," the hard voice said. "But if you try to lift the blindfold, if you even look up, you will be beaten. You don't know what it is to be beaten—you have no idea. If you disobey us in any way, we will not hesitate. You are nothing to us. Now you may eat."

The Superstars turned and walked away. The door opened, then closed. The other one stayed, the one who'd brought the food. I heard a small creak, like of a wooden chair, when he sat down. I could hear him breathing. So, a guard. Over by the door.

I ate the naan, drank the tea. And I began to be sure: the voice from above the Superstars was Amal's. At first I thought it wasn't because he sounded so different, like he was acting hard and tough. Or maybe it was acting when he'd been friendly and smooth. Whichever was the real him, it *was* him. I wondered how he kept his sneakers so clean, in a dirty old city like this.

When I was finished, the guard took my tray. He opened the door and I heard low voices; then he was back, the chair squeaking again as he sat. But now I had to use the toilet. I tried to ignore it, but it got bad. I cleared my throat; when the guard grunted, I pointed at myself, toward my butt. The guard made a sound like he was disgusted. But he got up, sighing heavily, and came over. I saw leather sandals. The guard untied me from the bed. Then he yanked on the rope, pulling me up.

Jerking at my leash, he led me down what I thought was a narrow hallway. He opened a door with a creak, and a stench hit me.

He unwrapped my hands. Pushed me into the smell. Shut the door.

Looking around through the bottom of my blindfold, I could see the space was tiny. There was a small sink, and a floor of stained white tiles that led to a dirtier white rectangle—a small sort of platform, like an inch above the floor, with a hole in the middle and a raised footprint on each side. I'd heard about this kind of toilet, but I hadn't seen one. The Royal Hotel had regular toilets. A roll of pink toilet paper sat on the tile by the platform.

A wave of awfulness rolled through me. What was I *doing* here? How could this be happening? How could I *use* this? But I had to.

Had to.

It was hard to keep my balance. Trying to get low enough, I almost fell over. The stench was horrible, I wanted to puke. But I did it; I did what I had to do, tilting and teetering on the footprints. And then I started to cry.

No! I would *not* let them get to me, I would not let them win.

I buckled my belt, rinsed my hands in the sink and knocked on the door. When the guard let me out, I stepped into the hall, then waited with dignity while he retied my hands.

I was lying down again when Amal came back. I heard footsteps up the stairs, then his shoes came in.

"Sit up! Do not speak. Sit up straight," he said. When I had worked my way back up, he said, "Here are your offenses. Do not talk, only listen."

He started talking in what seemed, this time, like a third voice. Like a bad teacher lecturing.

"First, you tried to corrupt good Muslims with Western pop music. This filth offends our faith, and you pushed it onto a Muslim boy—and far worse, onto a Muslim girl. We know this. We saw you place headphones on the Afghan boy, and we know you gave Western pop music to a good Pashtun girl. Your music is filthy pollution. This is your first offense.

"Second, you betrayed us. You agreed to assist our cause—but you lied, didn't you? You said you were one of us, then you betrayed us. Some brothers could be in jail right now, in some rat-infested hole you cannot even imagine. This is paradise compared to a Pakistani jail. You would have condemned the most faithful of believers to such a place? You are less than a dog to us. *Do not speak.*

"Finally, and this is worst by far, you aligned yourself with a scheme to glorify idolatry—to proclaim to the world that this base for our pure cause is a home of repulsive idol worship. Would you like to know the punishment for idolatry where I come from, in Saudi Arabia? Do not answer, I will tell you. It is beheading. So—three offenses, each one worse than the last.

"Why should we not kill you? To do this would be nothing to us—it would bring us merit for the world to come. We are here to fight evil, so why not start with you?

"We *should* do this—but first we will have a conversation, you and I. You will tell me everything you know about this scheme to spread idolatry—and I mean everything."

I thought, *Like what? What do I know that you don't?*

"Now we will go into a small room. A secure room," Amal said. "And we will not come out until you have told me everything. Believe me, you will do this. Let me show you why."

He walked over where the guard sat, then came back. He was holding something now, down where I could see it.

"Do you know what this is?"

It was a long rod. A baton, like the ones that some of Rasheed's friends were holding at the shrine. But it was bamboo, I could see now. Thick bamboo.

"They call this a *lathi,*" Amal said. "The police use it often." He tapped it against his palm. "It can make a strong impression."

He straightened up. Turned away. "Is the room ready?"

"It is ready," the guard said. I didn't know he spoke English.

"Two chairs? More rope? Two buckets, one with water?"

"Yes. Ready."

"We must have total security—*no one* is to disturb us. You understand?"

"Yes," the guard said.

"If anyone even comes near that room, I will be very angry. This is clear?"

"Of course."

"All right. Untie him. Leave the hands bound."

The guard came over, stooped and released me from the bed. Amal said, "Stand. Now walk." He pushed me, first in the back and then in the shoulder, turning me. Down the hall he pushed a door open, and moved me through it.

When he'd shut the door, Amal took my wrists and led me to a chair. "Sit," he said. When I had, he lifted off the blindfold.

I was in a small room. There was another chair, and two buckets on the floor. Amal started pacing back and forth. I still heard the street sounds, but muffled because now we were deeper inside.

Amal yanked up the lathi; he pointed it back the way we'd come, where the guard was. "These guys may not be real warriors, not yet. But out there"—he pointed—"over the mountains, *they are.* They are fighting in rags, risking everything. And I will *not*"—he slammed the baton on the table, *bam! BAM!*—"I will *not* let you destroy their chances!

"I will *not* let you lose this war," he yelled. He was being weirdly loud. "I *will not!* Do you understand me?"

I gaped at him. "Um...no. What?"

"No, of course you don't understand. You have no *idea* what you've done."

He sat down heavily. He stared at me and sighed, like I was the biggest problem in his life.

"You may as well hear the story," he said.

18.

Gunships

"PICTURE IT," AMAL SAID. "One single Afghan has climbed high on a mountainside."

He was talking in a new way, now. Maybe like himself this time.

"All the way up he has carried—and you can believe this, about these guys—a heavy machine gun. It is one of the very few the mujahideen possess. He has carried it up the mountain by himself."

"Okay..."

"Now comes a Soviet helicopter—a heavily armed, heavily armored Hind. If the Afghan shoots at the gunship from below, even a machine gun is useless, it cannot punch through the armor on its belly. But the Hind is hunting rebels on the ground. It flies low; the *mujahid* sits up high. With one burst from above the gunship, he destroys it. Boom.

"But these Hinds hunt in pairs. So the second comes in, also low—and the Afghan shoots *that* one down. These are ten-million-dollar machines, okay? And just before he was hit, the second pilot radioed back to base. *There's trouble here. Send a team.* The Russians dispatch twenty special-forces commandos, in a transport helicopter—and the mujahid shoots *that* down!

"Now the Russian radio traffic is frantic. All this damage done by one guy! And as it happens, *your* government is listening.

"I should not tell you any of this. You should not *be* here—but you are." He sighed. "So these transmissions are intercepted and translated in Washington, D.C. Some very important people in your Congress are now listening to Russians going crazy about an Afghan with *one* decent weapon. This finally convinces them."

"Convinces them what? I don't get it."

"Of course you don't. You have stumbled into what could be a turning point in history, and you have *no* idea what is happening. Why should you?"

He started pacing again. "Why *are* you here?"

"My dad made me come. You think I wanted to?"

"That doesn't matter. What you've done could destroy *everything*."

He grabbed the baton and slammed it on the table. *WHAM!*

"That was for them," he said.

"Huh?"

"For them. If they think I'm hurting you, punishing you, they will leave us alone."

Who *was* this guy?

"My government and yours have struck a bargain," Amal said. "Every dollar the U.S. sends to help the mujahideen, Saudi Arabia matches it. The Soviet Union is your big enemy, and your government likes that the Afghans are fighting the Soviets. But why should *my* government care?"

He stared at me, like I should know. "I don't know," I said.

"Soviet forces in Afghanistan are just a few hundred miles from Saudi Arabia," he said. "That is too close! And they are even closer to a narrow ship's passage called the Strait of Hormuz. Do you know what this is?"

I shook my head. If this was a quiz, I had a fat zero so far.

"Supertankers move through this passage full of the oil that my country ships to the world," he said. "This is the petroleum that keeps everyone's engines running. Especially your American cars.

"If the Soviets can conquer Afghanistan, they could advance to this passage—and take it. Then they could shut off the world's oil supply"—he snapped his fingers—"like *that*.

"But these crazy Afghans in their rags and sandals, they are tormenting the great Red Army. They don't give up! If we can just send them some powerful weapons, and maybe some warm coats and boots, they *might* stop the bear in his tracks. If they do, the whole world would be safer. *Now* do you see?"

"Who *are* you?" I said.

He slammed the baton, *BAM!* "That's not important."

"You're a spy. Some kind of spy. Right?"

BAM!

"I will tell you only what you need to know," he said. "So listen. Until now, your government has sent the rebels only a few hundred cheaply made AK-47 rifles. Smuggled them into Peshawar. This was nothing, but no one in D.C. believed the Afghans had a chance. Then comes this radio intercept. Hearing this, suddenly these guys in Washington get it."

He was pacing, pacing.

"And this Afghan has only a machine gun! That's not even close to what the U.S. *could* provide. So now there is serious talk in Washington of sending forty million dollars in secret aid to the rebels. This would include new Stinger missiles, powerful and portable. These can blow Hinds out of the sky—from *any* angle. They can change everything.

"And now *you* come along," he said. He lifted the baton again.

BAM!

"Suddenly we have this American boy, taken as a hostage. *Kidnapped!* These kids who've come to Peshawar, thinking they'll fight some holy war"—he waved toward the front—"they are fools. They're boys who want to be heroes, so they've done this stupid, *stupid* thing because they're mad at you. And this infernal city is infested with journalists! They're bored, looking for a *story*.

"If word gets out that some group connected to the Afghan rebellion has kidnapped an American teenager—*then* do you think the Americans will send their forty million? Of course not! They think life is precious, if it's an *American* life.

"So Washington will abandon the Afghans. Their cause will be lost—and maybe then the Soviet empire grabs for that chokehold on the world."

"You work for the Saudi government," I said. "Right? They sent you to keep tabs on that group. Their money guy is Saudi, right? That bin Laden guy."

"You are right about the second part," Amal said. "The first part is none of your business."

"What's your real name?"

"*Stop asking questions!*" He waved the lathi in my face. "Every second is precious. We have to *solve* this problem."

"We?"

"Yes—you and I. Everything depends on it. And these guys must believe I am interrogating you, being tough with you. So I raise my voice: *You will TELL me! You will tell me EVERYTHING!*"

BAM!

He sat down, heavily. "I cannot release you. These idiots would never allow it, and even trying to do that would expose my...situation. Luckily for us, the jihadis think your government is the devil, so they have not yet contacted U.S. authorities, to demand ransom or whatever. If the U.S. government hears about this, our whole cause is lost."

I thought about the note I'd left for my dad. I didn't know where Rasheed was—but Yusuf would be back at the Royal by now. The chokidar would have told Assad that men in a white Toyota took me. He might even know whose Toyota it was. Yusuf knew for sure.

"My dad and Rasheed's father—they'll know by now who's got me," I said.

"We have sent word to them," he said. "They know that if they alert the American or the Pakistani government, you will be killed. They are doing nothing, for now."

I stared at him. "So," I said. "Now what?"

"We are hoping for a resolution—a quick one. Do you know *any*one?"

"What do you mean?"

"I need a contact—someone I can approach very quietly, who can act as a go-between. Someone both sides can trust, who understands the gravity of this. This needs to be someone I can call on the phone. I cannot take the risk of a meeting."

"Hmm. Interesting."

"Why are you smiling?" he asked.

I turned on the bed, a bit. "Reach into my back pocket, on this side," I said, motioning with my head. "I'm pretty sure it's still in there." *God, I hope so,* I thought.

His forehead wrinkled, but then he came up close, and I felt his hand explore the pocket. He grunted. Now he was holding up a small white card.

He peered at it. "Does this man know you?"

"Yep."

"How do *you* know a police inspector?"

I shrugged. "Call the number," I said.

Amal nodded. He stood up. "In the meantime, there is something I must do. Before I can bring you back out there. Remove your shoes. Lie down on this table. Show the bottoms of your feet."

I just stared at him. He picked up the lathi.

"You have no choice," he said, "and neither do I. This interrogation must be convincing. And screams of pain you cannot fake."

I didn't fake them. Believe me.

19.
Midnight

DANISHA CONTACTED YUSUF through a letter delivered by rickshaw. Together they made their plan.

That night, when things were quiet and there was only one guard outside the hostage's door, Dani entered the building through a back door. She wore a dark burqa. She had sworn she would never wear one— but only a cloaked woman could enter the building uninspected. Also, a burqa's shapelessness was good for hiding things.

Dani's hid a tear-gas canister. It had been supplied by Prosecuting Sub-Inspector Shabbir Ahmad. Through contacts the police had, he had been able to find out where the hostage was being held.

The sleepy guard outside the building, his rifle drooping, did not even grunt. He would not acknowledge a female in a burqa, shuffling into the dark alley beside the building he was guarding. Dani walked down the alley, slipped through a rear door, and started up some stairs in dim yellow light.

She was afraid but determined. She would prove a Pashtun woman could be as brave and bold as a man. So she mounted the stairs softly, timidly, the way a woman in a burqa would.

Inside a darkly shuttered building across the lane, Sub-Inspector Ahmad and several other armed policemen waited silently along with Yusuf. The Afghan boy's head was wrapped in a bandage, and he carried an AK-47.

Dani reached the landing of the damp and ancient staircase. She could barely see, and only straight ahead. If she had to move fast, the *meshed eye slit of this infuriating sack might shift and she'd be blinded along with suffocated. Still, she was determined.*

In one pocket of the shalwar kameez beneath her burqa, she had the can of tear gas. In the other was a flashlight. In a few seconds she would open the door to the apartment, trigger the gas can, roll it in, then find a window she could open and give the signal— two quick flashes—to tell the police to make their move. With sudden overwhelming force, the cops would disarm the guard. If he resisted, they would shoot. Then they would storm upstairs, overpower the gas-disabled guard or guards, burst into the inner room and free the hostage.

It would all be over in less than a minute.

IF nothing went wrong.

Yet again, Dani's mind went over what might go wrong. The intelligence could be faulty. The presence of the guard outside seemed to say this was the right building, but what if this door led into the wrong apartment? What if there were armed guards, not only behind this door but inside the inner, hostage room as well? What if the guards stopped her, or shot her, before she could roll in the gas can?

She shut down all these thoughts and focused. Silently, with a steady hand, she lifted the heavy hem of the burqa and extracted the gas canister from her pocket. She prepared to release the trigger and, in one smooth motion, open the door...

Wait. How do you trigger a tear-gas canister?

I had never seen one. Well, maybe in a movie. I had the idea it was shaped like a tin can, with a sort of neck or nozzle at the top. The gas came spraying, or shooting, whatever gas does, out of that part.

Sure, but is there a trigger? Or would she just unscrew the cap?

I lay there in the dark. Sharp and burning pain pulsed through the bottoms of my feet where Amal had whacked them, over and over. It was the middle of the night; the pain kept waking me up. But I'd had the scene going good in my mind. I would think this part through, then I'd imagine the whole scenario again. It was something to do. Like watching a movie in my mind.

She unscrewed the cap on the canister. And just as the gas—is it colored? or like gray? say rose-colored, that's good—started to escape, she squelched the coughing reflex, twisted the doorknob…

Wait. Wouldn't the door be locked? Damn…okay, say it's not locked, because with armed guards, you wouldn't need…

But wait—there was a guard *outside* the door to the apartment. He was out there now. I think he smoked. Every once in a while I heard him cough.

Damn.

I just lay there. I couldn't see anything, I couldn't think of anything. And my feet were on fire.

Fantasy only keeps you happy for a while.

In the cold, dismal morning I lay with bound hands clutching a thin gray blanket close around my chest. I was waiting for something to eat, listening to my hollow stomach complain. Last night they gave me a naan and *kabob,* chunks of grilled meat from the bazaar, wrapped in newspaper with blotchy grease stains. I didn't know how to eat it. The guard showed me to tear off a chunk of the naan, fold it and use it to pick up the meat. You popped the folded chunk in your mouth. It was fairly decent, actually.

But this morning no meat. They just brought a naan, plus gray tea with little grease globules floating in it. My feet were still sore, but they were getting better and at least the blindfold was gone. Amal had grunted an order to leave it off.

Even so, the shutters to the outside world were closed tight, and they kept my hands tied to the bed. Really nice guys.

What could my dad and Assad do? They were teachers, they had no money. And what—I kept thinking these questions, they churned in my head—what did these guys *want?*

Would they kill me?

If they did, what would happen to my dad? And my mom?

What happens when you're dead? How can anyone know? Rasheed said holy warriors go to paradise—but if there is a paradise, I was pretty damn positive you don't get there by killing people.

It was so frustrating and infuriating to not be able to *do* anything. To not be able to walk around the room or go to the bathroom, unless you beg for permission and wait for them to untie you, *if* they feel like it. This morning when I had to go, the guard was outside. I'd heard him go down the stairs, probably to smoke. I yelled, "Hey. *Hey!*"

Then I heard footsteps running up; the door blasted open and the guard snatched up the lathi. He waved it at me, over my head like he could crack my skull with it, like he so much wanted to. So I didn't yell anymore. Except on the inside.

That's how it was. The pressure would build and build. I sat or lay there, clutching my blanket, the tension like a steel band tightening around my chest. I could hardly breathe. There was nothing to do about it, and nowhere for any of it to go.

So I waited for food. They didn't give me anything for lunch. After hours and hours, my stomach felt like it had crawled up into my chest when finally, after dark had come into the room, after the guard had switched on the one lightbulb that hung on a cord from the ceiling, they brought me a naan and kabob in grease-spotted newspaper.

Amal came in when the food did, though he didn't handle it. He never did. He had on the spotless Adidas, plus a preppy blue shirt and jeans ironed to a sharp crease.

As the guard laid the dinner beside me on the bed, Amal stood behind him and nodded to me. Just once. Then he turned and walked back out, down the stairs and gone.

Sitting there chewing and thinking, I wondered if the nod meant he had contacted the inspector. He had wanted me to know, right? I thought and thought.

Then, after a while, I started to notice that something seemed different.

It was hard to understand what it was. The room was the same, the one lightbulb was the same, and I was pretty sure the guard outside the door hadn't gone downstairs for a cigarette...but something was different.

It was outside that was different. It wasn't that something was happening...something *wasn't* happening.

The street sounds weren't there. Or maybe they were there but they had faded, like they were farther away. Why? I didn't know, but I tried hard to listen.

The honking horns and the engine noise, the small blatting engines and the big, barging ones—I could still hear them, but more like...background. Farther away. I could almost hear some softer sounds, but I couldn't tell what they were. Like really low murmuring, and maybe shuffling around.

But really, it was quiet. That's what was strange.

And then:

BOOM!

20.

Festival

AGAIN:

BOOM!

Outside the door, a chair was shoved back into a wall and feet pounded down the stairs.

BOOM!

BOOM!

BOM BOM BOM!

Not explosions. Drums.

Loud drums.

Really loud drums.

bada bom BOM

bada bom BOM

bada bom BOM BOM

bada bom BOM BOM

bada bom *BOOM!*

bada bom *BOOM!*

bada bom BOOM BOOM

bada bom *BOOM!*

Every huge line ended in a deep-bass explosion—and now I heard voices out in the stairwell, and footsteps hammering up the stairs. What was happening? Who was out there?

The door blasted open. Four young guys with wispy beards came in yelling and arguing. They were the guards and they were confused—they were yelling. At each other.

bada bom BOM BOM

bada bom BOM BOM

bada bom *BOOM!*

bada bom *BOOM!*

bada bom BOM BOM

bada bom BOM BOM

bada bom *BOOM!*

bada bom *BOOM!*

There were *lots* of drummers out there—and they were playing really big, really loud drums. It was thunderous, pounding. It was loud as *hell.*

bada bom BOM BOM

bada bom BOM BOM

bada bom *BOOM!*

bada bom *BOOM!*

The Wahhabis were *upset.* After they'd argued with each other and yelled at each other and stalked around the room for a few minutes, they rushed back out in a bunch, like four stooges shoving together through a door.

Their steps thundered down and out. I heard one of them sit down heavily on the chair just outside. The rhythm outside changed, got more insistent:

BOOM badalak BOOM BOOM badalak

BOOM BOOM badalak BOOM BOOM! badalaka

BOOM BOOM badalaka BOOM BOOM badalak

bap dabap BOOM!

bap dabap BOOM!

It was like they'd thundered out their opening and now they were digging into a groove. A *huge* groove. It was loud as a rock concert, but not the same. Some of the drums were now clacketing out higher rhythms that got more and more complex and jazzy, but they all still pounded the bass notes together:

badalak *BOOM BOOM*

badalaka *BOOM BOOM*

bap dabap *BOOM!*

bap dabap *BOOM!*

This went on. I mean on and *on,* making my hanging lightbulb sway and pulse. It wasn't my music, it was theirs—funky and cool, very very loud and *never* letting up.

Never.

After they'd pounded out one jam for a while, the drummers would finally stop—and when they did, people would clap. I heard laughter, shouting, clapping, hooting... then the players would start again. A little different this time, but every time *loud.*

dabap dabap da BOM BOM

dabap dabap da BOM BOM

dap dap

BOM BOM!

dap dap

BOOM!

dap dap

BOOM!

I heard voices in the stairwell, urgent. I heard the guard thump down those stairs, and a door down there slammed.

And then my light went out.

21.

Dark Passage

I WAS STILL TIED to the bed. It was pitch dark, and outside the drums were still thundering and bass-exploding, but in here I was more and more sure I was alone.

Rashi's gang was gone.

So I started to yell.

"Hey! Hey! *Hey!*"

Bapa dom BOM BOM bapa dom BOM BOM

"*Hey! HEY! Hey Wasi! HEY, WASI!*"

I had to time my yells to the second-long pauses between drumming phrases.

Bapa dom BOM BOM bapa dom BOM BOM

"Hey I'm in here they're gone *GET ME OUT!* **HEY!**"

And then someone was coming up the stairs. More than one.

"Hey! In here!"

The door opened. It was dark in the hall. But there was movement—maybe two or three people, darker than the dark. I heard a scratch; a match lit up. The figures came in, and the one holding the match reached up to the little chain hanging from the lightbulb. Pulled it down. Nothing.

A burst of talking. I heard the word "power." The match went out.

Another scratch, another light: the person came close, and pulled at the rope between my bound wrists and the bed. Burst of talking. Two of them went back down the stairs. The match went out again.

"Don't worry," said a voice I knew.

"Yusuf!"

"Yes. They are going for a knife. To cut this."

He sat beside me on the bed.

"Dude," I said. "Those drums are *loud*."

He chuckled. "They are outdoor drums."

"I'm pretty sure Rashi's friends ran away," I said.

"Maybe they cut the power," he said. "They are gone?"

"Yeah—you blew their minds, man. How'd you *find* me? How did you know where I was?"

The drums erupted, and footsteps came upstairs. A flashlight opened a cone of light, and now a young man was kneeling before us, slipping a knife carefully between my wrist and the rope. He turned the knife, and started sawing at the rope.

"There is something those guys don't know," Yusuf said.

"What?"

"A secret can be kept in Peshawar for a day. *Maybe* two." I saw his eyes, just outside the cone of light. "But no longer."

The back of the blade moved back and forth against my wrist. The triple-wound rope was fraying, fraying...

And I was free.

"Let's go," Yusuf said. He took my hand and led me—I was kind of shaky—down the stairs. At the bottom he pushed open a door, and hand in hand we stepped outside.

Two Old City lanes joined here at a T, one running across and the one we stood on ending at the T—and people were everywhere. Ranks of drummers filled the street ahead of us. Hanging from cords around their necks they all had much bigger versions of my drum, and each drummer was playing with two sticks. One stick racketed out fast rhythms on the smaller end; the other, bent like a hockey stick, pounded out the bass. I mean *pounded*.

Crowds of men and boys filled the edges and thronged the side streets in the dark. Some were playing instruments, but most were just hanging out. As we stepped out and stood there, the drum chorus came suddenly to a huge end:

backeta backeta BOM BOM
backeta backeta BOM BOM
backa-dacka-dacka-dacka
BOOM!

The drummers all raised their sticks high—and in the dark the street exploded with yelling and shouting and cheers.

Wasil stepped out from the first row of all these drummers. He came toward us, slipped off a small backpack, reached into it...and handed me a tambourine.

"It is for you, from us," he said. "Play with us!"

He lifted one arm, like to start everyone again, but I said, "Wasi. Wait."

His arm stayed up. "Yes?"

"What do you call that drum?"

"The *dhol.* These are festival drums!"

"How did you *do* this?"

"Every drummer in Peshawar is here. Every one!"

"But *how*?"

"Pir Sahib has said, all musicians come. We must bring *all* the music!"

He dropped his arm, and they all started.

backa backa BOM BOM
backa backa BOM!

He stepped back and joined in. I looked at my tambourine, but Yusuf took my hand again and pulled. He was pulling hard; I had to follow.

He led us onto the lane that went off to the right, and in the dark we threaded, along its outer edge, through the celebrating crowd. Men's faces swam up as they slapped me on the back, stuck out hands for me to shake. In the dark and in glimmers of light, we passed faces, mustaches, turbans, rolled caps, faces and faces—nods and smiles and laughter, glimpsed and gone as Yusuf pulled me along.

"Where are we going?" I yelled at the back of his head.

"Just come!"

We ducked down a murky alley. By now the clamor and thundering, the clapping and the clattering had faded behind us. Just my tambourine clacked softly to the rhythm of our steps.

22.
Do Not Look

I'M SITTING ON AN OLD COUCH in a small living room. I'm alone in here, staring at a small television on a cheap metal stand. It's showing old American wrestling, in black and white with the sound off.

Yusuf brought me through the front door of this place and left me, saying he'd be outside. The door is shut now to the dark alley outside. I can still faintly hear the clamoring jam in the distance. In here it's quiet, except that just beyond the open inner doorway that seems to lead into the rest of the house, I hear whispers.

They're almost not there, except that...they are. Vague, shimmery whispers.

I'm sitting, waiting, unsure. Yusuf explained nothing. I don't know what's happening. So far, except for the whispers, nothing has.

A boy appears in the inner doorway, from somewhere inside the house. He's holding a tray with tea and biscuits. They're the same simple, rectangular biscuits that Pir Sahib gave me in his shop.

I've never seen this boy before. He's maybe eleven. He sets the tray down. Then he goes.

It has been several minutes and no one else has appeared or said a word to me, so I stare at the wrestling. I eat a cookie. Gratefully, I drink the tea. And as I do, I become aware that faces, the eye-tops of faces, are sliding out along the near edge of the inner doorway.

Looking at me.

Maybe two or three faces. I never see them; when I look they are gone. I look to the TV and they—I sense them, am aware of the shapes—reappear. I flick my eyes back but they're gone. There is the vaguest hint of giggling. Nothing more. Then there's a soft shuffling, as if the girls, they must be girls, have slipped deeper into the house.

Now I'm alone.

And now she speaks.

"I'm so glad you're free," she says.

"What? Dani? Where are—"

"No. Stay there."

"I don't understand."

"This is a Pashtun home."

"Okay. Whose?"

"A friend's. It does not matter—but this is a traditional home, and this the only way we can talk. You must not even look around the corner. If you look, I will have to disappear, and you will have to leave. And you will never see me again."

"What? *Why?*"

"Because you're leaving Peshawar," Dani says. "Our fathers are arranging the flight. I think tonight."

"To*night?*"

"I think so."

"But our dads don't know I'm out. I just *got* out."

A pause. "They know," she says. "As soon as you leave here, you must take a rickshaw to the hotel. They are waiting for you there."

"But how could they—"

"Luke, please. It's best if they explain."

"Explain what?"

"The important thing is, you are free. And you're going home."

"Okay. Okay. So are you coming?"

"Coming?"

"Yeah—to America. With us. You're coming, right?"

"Luke…"

"Wait—have you run away? Don't run, Dani. Come with us. We can *do* it."

"Luke. Please stop."

"Oh. Sorry."

"It's all right, but try to understand. My brother has gone. My father has lost...a lot."

"Um...okay..."

"So I will stay. With my family."

"But *why*? What'll happen?"

"I don't know," she says. "But this is our city. Our country. Why should we run away?"

"But you wouldn't be running away—you'd get an education. You'd have a career. You'd have a *life*." I'm almost pleading now.

She is silent. The house is silent. The wrestling is silent.

"I can't leave them," she finally says. "Not now. I don't know what will happen. But Luke, when things are hard...women stay. We just do. I don't know how to explain."

"But..."

"Please, Luke. I know it's not what you wanted, but...try to understand."

Something's pounding inside me. "So," I say, "you got me to come here...so you could tell me?"

"That's right. Out of respect, do you see it? And...I know there's more, but we can't talk about it. Not here. And, Luke—you're going to have to go. They're waiting for you."

"But how did you *do* this? How did we get to be here?"

"I sent word to your friend, at the hotel. He helped me. He understands."

"He's a good man," I say. "Do you still want to teach? I mean, do you..."

"Of course—I want to get my secondary school certificate. I want to go to college. I *have* to go."

"But they could kill you."

"Maybe. But only maybe."

I think she'll say more, but there's only silence.

"Luke, you have to go," she finally says. "They need to see you.

They need to know you're okay. This is very hard for them."

"But...are *you* okay?"

"Yes. Sure. We have to say goodbye now."

"But, Dani...can we write? Or something?"

"Maybe. I don't know what will happen. But, Luke...I will always remember."

I gulp. Swallow hard. "Me too," I say.

"Your friend is waiting outside. And, Luke?"

"Uh?"

"Happy Christmas."

"What?"

"Don't you know? This is your Christmas Eve."

I'm stunned. "It is?"

"It is."

"Then...wait. I want to give you something."

"Luke..."

"No—it's Christmas, okay? It's what we do."

I reach around, for the only thing I have. The tambourine jingles just slightly as I slide it along the floor, very carefully into the opening. There's a shimmer of whispering, back in there somewhere.

"Luke, please. You don't have to..."

"No—I want to. The drummers gave me this, back there."

"Then it is yours, their gift to you. This is a big thing—you must keep it."

"Well...but it's all I've got on me. I can't..."

"Wait," she says. "Just one second."

I hear movement, rustling. Shimmers. Rustling again. And now the tambourine is slid back into the opening.

I almost see her fingers; I close my eyes, so that I won't. It's a Pashtun home.

When I open my eyes, the tambourine is lying there.

"Now it has a gift from me, too," says her voice, the last time I hear it.

I pick up the instrument. Turn it over.

On the bottom, on the skin, in felt-tip pen, she has written:

PLAY

23.
The Trade

THE MUSIC SOUNDS WERE GONE. "Are they done playing?" I asked Yusuf as we started up the narrow street, in the murk of the city's night.

"I think so," he said as he led me past a line of empty wooden carts, the flat-topped kind that held pyramids of oranges and bananas in the daytime. "They have done what they came to do."

"But how did you *do* that?" I asked, stumbling to keep up. "How did you get them all there?"

"I didn't—I only spoke to Pir Sahib at his shop, and to your friend Wasil in Dabgari Bazaar. There are too many musicians in Peshawar just now, local players and guys from Afghanistan. I think your friend knows them all—and everyone respects Pir Sahib. When he says something must be done, people tell each other."

"Word spreads fast," I said. "Like you said."

"Yes. And also...people know what you did."

"What I did?"

"Yes. That you traded yourself," he said. "I think everyone in Peshawar knows."

"*Everyone?*"

He shrugged. "Half of the city was there tonight."

"Half the guys, you mean."

He nodded. "But I think the others, the women and the kids... they heard, too. People will remember."

I didn't know what to say. "Um…how's your head?"

"It is fine. Pashtuns have hard heads."

"You don't have to tell me."

As we turned a corner I heard new sounds, and suddenly we were in a really big space—a huge open plaza, with lights and shops around the edges and traffic pushing by, even at whatever time this was.

"Isn't this…"

"Yes—Qissa Khwani Bazaar. The Street of Storytellers." He waved, and a rickshaw pulled up. "Quickly," Yusuf said. "Your father is waiting."

Looking through the glass of the hotel's front door, I saw police in there. I saw people pacing. Then the people saw me.

A guy behind the desk leaned over to yell into the dining room— and then my dad was running out, Assad behind him. Now I was lifted off the ground, my dad spinning me round and round.

"Oh my God my God my God," he said, setting me down. "Let me *see* you."

"I may throw up."

"Try not to. You don't look too bad. Are you okay?"

Sub-Inspector Ahmad came out the front door. Assad was shaking my hand, hugging me too. Hugging me hard.

"Did they hurt you?" my dad asked. "I just want to know. Did they hit you?"

I shrugged. My shoulder still ached a little and my feet were sore, but no big deal.

"Not really. I'm glad Yusuf's okay."

"He has seen worse," Assad said.

"I know."

"Everyone, please—come inside," the inspector said. "Quickly."

He herded us in. They sat me down at the first table in the dining room. The cop sat across. My dad sat next to me, Assad on the other side.

"I must ask you some questions—please don't mind," the inspector said. "Do you know where you were held?"

I glanced back at Yusuf, who said something in Pashto.

"Where the musicians came," I said.

They looked at me. The inspector said, "Musicians?"

"Yeah—the drummers. That's how I got out."

The men exchanged looks. They seemed puzzled.

"Many dhol players came there," Yusuf told them. "To celebrate when he was released."

I said, "No, they *got* me released."

Yusuf shrugged.

"I don't get it," I said.

"The important thing is, you're okay," my dad said. Assad nodded.

The inspector asked, "Have you seen Professor Shaheen's son? Rasheed? He is missing."

I looked at Assad. Oh no.

"Um…I saw him…yesterday morning, when they got me," I said to him. "At your house."

"But why did you come there?" Assad asked. "So early?"

"Um, I was trying…to find Yusuf."

"And you spoke to Rasheed?"

"Yes. He said he was going into training. For…you know, jihad."

They looked at each other. The inspector nodded, then turned to me and said, "We have strongly advised that you and your father leave the city—depart Pakistan on the first flight tomorrow morning. We cannot force you, but in the circumstances…"

"That's right." My dad laid a hand on my shoulder. "We're going home, son."

"But…are you done? You guys have to finish your work," I said. "I mean, that's what this was all about."

They looked at each other. It bothered me that they kept doing that.

"These people have done something new in Peshawar—made

a kidnapping, taken a hostage," the inspector said. "Even worse, they snatched an American. This could have created an international incident. But with the cooperation of your father and Professor Shaheen, we were able to deal with the situation quietly. And quickly."

Before I could ask anything, the inspector stood up. He shook hands with the two professors.

"Thank you, gentlemen," he said. "How soon can you be ready?" he asked my dad.

"Give us an hour," my dad said. "Luke needs to pack."

Shabbir Ahmad nodded. "We will send a car. A secure vehicle, do not worry."

He started to walk toward the front door, then he turned back. "I'm very sorry," he said to them. I didn't get why he would say that, but then he turned and walked through the lobby. A uniformed cop followed him out.

"Luke, come upstairs—you need to pack," my dad said, heading for the stairs. "You can say your goodbyes after you're ready." He walked up the stairs. I followed.

"We're spending the night at the American Consulate, just to be safe," he said as we walked to our rooms. "They have Marines there."

"But what about your book? Did you get it done? You couldn't have, right? I mean with all this."

My dad shook his head.

"So," I said, "are we bringing that stuff home? You can't leave it all here."

My dad opened the door to my room. My stuff was in there, jumbled up the way I'd left it that morning. The wrecked drum was on the bed; only Yusuf's bloody pajamas were gone. My dad walked past my stuff and opened the door between our rooms.

"Please," he said, turning back. "Pull everything together quickly—anything you want to take." Over his shoulder, I could see his room was neat. Just his shoulder bag on the bed, and beside it the typewriter, in its zipped-up case.

I said, "Did you pack it all? The book stuff?"

He leaned against the door frame, looking down, hands in his pockets.

I said, "Dad?"

He looked up, finally. "That's what this was about," he said. "That was the trade."

24.

Open Eyes

I SAT DOWN HARD. When I said "What?" it came out as a squeak.

"Luke," he said, "they were very clear. It was our project or you. The police advised us to take them seriously—and there was huge pressure put on Assad, here in Peshawar.

"Apparently it was really important, for some reason, that this not leak out, that the Americans in particular not find out about it. And the people who had you have an extreme ideology. They dehumanize anyone who isn't the narrowest of believers—even other Muslims.

"When they threatened to kill you, we had to believe them," he said. "The police said if this got out, if it became an international story, they might have killed you just to raise their own profile."

"Not to lose face," I said.

"Huh?"

"They couldn't just let me go. They'd have lost face." I shook my head, to clear it. "But…"

"Luke, there was only one choice."

"But, Dad. Your *work*. Professor Shaheen's work. All of it?"

He nodded. "That was the deal."

"But…you kept something, right? You kept a copy. A secret copy. I mean right?"

My dad shook his head.

"The Shaheens want to stay here, Luke. They're determined; this is their country. Part of the deal was that, along with giving them all we had, we promised we would never publish anything about the

Gandharan Buddhas, about what they call idolatry. Anything. If we did that, and the Shaheens are still here in Peshawar..."

I stood up, started pacing around the room. Back and forth. Standing in the doorway, he just watched.

"I can't believe it," I said. "Everything you've done? For like three years?"

"Longer, if you add it all up. But...yeah." He shook his head, slowly.

"But nobody will hear the story now," I said. "Nobody will *know*."

He shrugged. "But you'll grow up—you'll have a life. You'll *live*. Luke, what else was I supposed to do?"

I stared at him. I was slowly understanding what he'd done. I had no idea what to say. But then...I thought of something to do.

I went to my dresser. Opened the drawer, brought out something wrapped in a nest of newspaper.

I offered it to him. He peered at the wrapped thing.

I said, "Take it—but be really careful. Don't *drop* it." As he took it, and opened up the paper in his hand, I said, "Did you know it's Christmas Eve?"

"Well, yeah, but...oh my God. Luke. Where'd you *get* this?"

"From that old guy. At the ruin."

"You did? But he's not...they're not supposed to...oh, Luke. We shouldn't *have* this."

"I knew I wasn't supposed to, but...you need to take this home," I said. "You need to keep it."

He held it up. "See how the face is so young-looking, so lean in shape? It could be Greek, right? Only a true Gandharan Buddha looks like this. And, Luke, do you see how his eyes are wide open?"

"You know, I noticed that."

"Yes. From that and from this type of glittery stone, we can be pretty sure this is one of the earliest Buddhas made. It would have been carved, most likely, sometime between 100 and 200 A.D."

"Okay, Professor."

"It's been broken off a storytelling sculpture," he said. "There are lots of those in the museum. And the open eyes—they're a striking feature of the first Gandharan Buddhas. As the image spread along the trading pathways into the rest of the world, it became accepted to show the Buddha's eyes as sort of half-closed. Because he's meditating, right? Looking within.

"But the Gandharan images—the earliest ones, with the Greek and Indian influences coming together—show him with wide-open eyes. We thought that might be part of the message from Gandhara to the world. Look with open eyes, right? *See.*"

"Merry Christmas," I said.

"The nose is gone, but otherwise it's remarkably whole, considering that it lay in rubble for a thousand and a half years. It's wrong to take away Gandharan treasures, but..."

"Pack it up," I said. "You need to have it."

He shrugged. "I don't imagine they'll search us too closely. They just want to get us on a plane before something else happens." He studied the sculpture. His hand bobbed a little, like he was weighing it. Then he closed the newspaper nest in his hand.

"Luke, you need to get ready. Okay?"

"Yeah. But would you ask Yusuf to come up? Real quick?"

"Um...yeah, okay. But quick."

"Yeah. And, Dad?"

"Yes?"

"I know what you did. I mean, all this. I'll always know."

He frowned. "I almost got you killed."

"Well, there's that. What are we going to tell Mom?"

He made a pretty funny grimace. "I just hope she lets me live."

"Yeah."

"I'm serious."

"I know."

He smiled, shook his head. Turning to go, he called back: "Pack!"

"I'm packing!"

But I wasn't, not yet. I stood there looking at the rest of the things in my drawer.

When Yusuf came up, he had tea. A small pot on a tray. I was about to say, "Oh for God's sake," when I noticed there were two cups.

He set the tray down, and poured for us.

"Qawa," I said.

"Yes. It's okay?"

"Of course it's okay. I'm going to miss qawa."

We drank, sitting together on the bed.

"Yusuf, what about those drummers? I thought they were what got me out. I thought that was so cool."

"I think they were part of it," he said. "After I talked to Pir Sahib, he made it known that it was important to find out where you were."

"So what *happened*?"

He shrugged. "The professors and the police, they were not telling me much—but I think things were difficult. It is hard, to make a bargain like this. Then someone told someone where you were, and all the drummers went there—and very quickly, it was over. The Wahhabis were gone. Maybe no one knows all of it—but I think the music was part of it. They made pressure, and then there was a deal."

A knock on the door. "Luke?" my dad's voice asked. "Are you packing?"

"Yeah—be down in a minute."

We heard his footsteps go downstairs. I finished my tea.

"There's one more thing," I said to Yusuf. "Tonight and tomorrow —it's a holiday for us. In our culture."

"Yes. Your festival."

"Yeah. So at Christmas, we give presents. Gifts, right?"

He nodded. I went to my bed, and pulled the red case from the jumble there. Zipped it open, and pulled out Bob Marley's *Natty Dread, Exodus, Survival,* and *Uprising.* He didn't have those. I put them in his hand.

"These are for you."

His eyes got big. He looked at the cassettes. *"Tashakor,"* he said.

"Huh?"

"It means thank you."

"You're welcome. And I need to ask you to do something."

"Of course." He put his tapes on the tray. "Anything."

I put the red case in his hands. Eight tapes still in it. "Take this to Dabgari Bazaar. Give it to Wasi."

He grinned. "He will be very happy."

"Tell them thank you. For me. You could also copy these Bob tapes for him. I mean if you want to."

"Of course," Yusuf said. "I will."

"Um...what's that word? For thanks?"

"Tashakor."

"Right. So, tashakor. For everything."

"For nothing," he said. "I failed you."

"You did not."

"I did. You were under my protection."

"You didn't *fail* me. I wanted to go out that night."

"And then you traded yourself," he said. "That was foolish."

I grinned. "I'd do it again."

He stuck out his hand, and we shook. "You really are stubborn as a Pashtun," he said.

"Thank you very much."

I said it low, like Elvis Presley would have. I couldn't help myself.

There wasn't that much to pack, and I did it fast. Along with my stuff in the backpack, I had four things from here that I wanted to keep. One was the tambourine, wrapped in my dirty Bob shirt. The others were her letter, her note, and the Meena cassette.

When I was ready, I stopped at the door and took one look back, so I could remember this room. I was leaving only one thing behind. In the top drawer of the bureau was Rasheed's pamphlet on jihad.

25.

Tashakor

WHEN I CAME DOWN to the dining room, only Assad was there, sitting alone at a table. I didn't see my dad. A couple of cops were standing over by the lobby, but around the professor there was only empty space. I looked at him, and saw how much he had lost. His life's work. His only son.

I went over, and quietly set down my backpack. And the broken drum.

He looked up. "Your father is taking care of the hotel charges," he said softly. "This may take a minute."

"That's okay," I said. "I...sort of don't know what to do with this."

I lifted the drum, set it on the table. Looking at it, Assad's eyes went wet. He wiped at them, embarrassed.

"I'm sorry," I said. "Those guys cut it."

He nodded. "My son's friends."

"Yeah."

He picked up the drum, and held it for a little while. Then he offered it back.

"You take it," he said. "You can get it fixed."

"I don't know how. Or who."

"Take it to the music department, at the college," he said. "They'll know what to do—and they will be very interested. Maybe someone there can give you lessons."

I shook my head, sadly. "I don't know who I'd play with. I sort of don't want to leave, now."

"After all this? You would stay?"

"Well...I don't know if I would *stay*, but I also don't totally want to leave."

He nodded. "When you open your heart to anything, you must know it can be broken. But to live with a closed heart...that is not to live at all."

"I'm so sorry about the project, Professor. And about Rasheed. I hope he'll be okay."

His mouth tightened. "The rumor is that those men have set up a training camp in the hills, somewhere near the border. To turn boys into jihadis. I think about going there—demanding that they give my son back to his family."

He shook his head. "But I don't know if the rumor is true, or where the camp would be. And if Rasheed has made a choice, then I must respect it. All young men must make choices. I only...well. Thank you for your good wishes."

The pressure was in me, building up. I had to say something.

"I wish the girls, the women...I wish they had more choices, too," I said.

He nodded. "So do I."

Now he looked at me. "My daughter is a brave young woman," he said. "I know she has made an impression."

"I hope she'll be okay," I said a little too quickly.

"I hope so, too," he said. "It's hard to know what will happen."

"I didn't mean...I mean I didn't..."

"It's all right," Assad said. "I only wish you had met again in better circumstances."

"Me too. And I'm...I'm really sorry," I said. "I mean that nobody'll get to hear the story you almost finished. About the Greeks and the Buddhas."

"The Buddhists. And that's not true! One person heard it."

"Who?"

"Why, you."

"Oh. Well…"

"You have this knowledge," the professor said. "You must sort this out for yourself—but you have it for a reason. I think all of this must have happened for a reason. I don't know what will become of us here—anyone can see we will have difficulties. And, young man, I will say this only once: we bought your life at great cost. Live it truly. Live it bravely. And please, do not forget the Shaheens."

My dad strode back in.

"Luke, are you ready? The car is here."

Assad stood, and so did I. We shook hands. Through the glass doors I could see a dark car, waiting. Beyond it was the crazy intersection, so full of noise and risk, where somehow people made way. Somehow they got through. Most of the time, anyway.

"Please keep in touch," I said to Assad.

He smiled. "Of course. Inshallah, our families will always know what happens to each other. Ah—here is your good friend."

Yusuf had come up quietly. He was standing with a small man in white pajamas.

"This is my father," Yusuf said.

The man looked up at me with bright eyes. He shook my hand. "Very happy to meet you, sir. Thanks to God you are safe."

I wasn't sure what to say, so we kept shaking hands. I finally said, "Your son is a good man. A good friend." The dad nodded, and stepped back by his son.

"We have something for you," Yusuf said.

He held out a rolled Pashtun cap.

"For you," he said. "From myself and my father—and my sister. From our family."

I took it. I put it on. It fit pretty good. "Tashakor," I said.

And one last time, we shook hands.

AFTERWORD

STREET OF STORYTELLERS is fiction, but the history, ancient and modern, in which the story is placed is real. Osama bin Laden's fatwa didn't actually happen. But here are some things that did, in the years that followed:

•

IN 1985, millions of dollars in secret aid and arms began flowing from the United States to the Afghan rebels. Among the armaments smuggled into Afghanistan during the next few years were nearly five hundred U.S.-made Stinger missile systems. With portable launchers and guidance systems that locked onto the heat in an aircraft, Stingers proved very effective against the armed jets and helicopters of the Soviet Union, which until then had dominated the fighting. According to a U.S. report, the mujahideen used Stingers to shoot down 269 Russian aircraft.

•

IN FEBRUARY 1987, the founder of the Revolutionary Association of the Women of Afghanistan, Meena Keshwar Kamal—known simply as Meena to many Afghan and Pakistani women—was assassinated in Quetta, Pakistan. She and her husband, who was murdered the year before, left three children. A fine book about her life is *Meena, Heroine of Afghanistan*. In 2002, two Afghan men confessed to the killing and were executed in Pakistan.

•

IN FEBRUARY 1989, the last Soviet Red Army unit pulled out of Afghanistan. Left in its wake were a number of rebel factions, which for the next several years struggled violently against each other to dominate a shattered country flooded with powerful weapons, many of them American-supplied.

•

IN NOVEMBER 1989, Abdullah Azzam, the Palestinian religious leader who had called on Muslims around the world to join the Afghan rebellion, was killed along with his two sons by a car bomb in Peshawar. No one was arrested for Azzam's murder. He and Osama bin Laden had come to disagree in a big way: Azzam wanted the jihadist organization they had created, now known as *al Qaeda,* or "the Base," to remain focused on Afghanistan, while bin Laden wanted to spread their campaign to other parts of the world.

•

IN 1996, after several years of violent chaos in much of Afghanistan, a religious extremist group known as the *Taliban* (or "students") took power in that devastated nation. The Taliban imposed a regime of nightmarish severity. Among other measures, girls' education was banned, women were forbidden to work outside the home, and all forms of music were outlawed.

•

IN MARCH 2001, two giant Buddhas carved into a cliff in the Bamiyan Valley of central Afghanistan were dynamited by the Taliban. The largest and most famous stone statues created by the ancient Gandharan civilization, the "Bamiyan Buddhas" were 175 and 120 feet tall, and had been designated a World Heritage Site by the United Nations. Taliban leaders said they were destroyed because they were idols.

•

ON SEPTEMBER 11, 2001, two civilian jetliners hijacked by al Qaeda militants flew into and destroyed the twin towers of the World Trade Center in New York City. A third jetliner was flown into the

Pentagon, headquarters of the U.S. military, in Washington, D.C. A fourth plane, apparently also heading for Washington, crashed into a field in Pennsylvania after passengers overwhelmed the hijackers. In all, 2,996 people died in the attacks.

•

IN THE AFTERMATH OF SEPTEMBER 11, American Special Forces helped an anti-Taliban coalition push the extremists out of power in Afghanistan. The United States worked with Afghans to set up a new system of government, with the nation's first constitution and democratic elections—but with secret support from the Pakistan military, the Taliban continued to fight. Operating at first mainly from the mountains along the Afghan-Pakistan border, the Taliban mounted a guerrilla war against a coalition of armed forces from several nations, led by the United States.

•

IN MARCH 2009, a bomb planted by Pakistani extremists severely damaged the shrine of Rahman Baba in Peshawar. A number of other Sufi shrines in Pakistan have also been damaged or demolished, sometimes with people killed, as militants use threats and explosives to discourage Pakistanis from attending these traditional centers of tolerance, compassion and music. But the Rahman Baba shrine has been rebuilt and it continues to attract many visitors, as do other Sufi shrines around the country.

•

ON MAY 2, 2011, Osama bin Laden, who had orchestrated the September 11 attacks as the leader of al Qaeda, was killed in a helicopter-borne U.S. assault on the home where he was hiding, within a walled compound in Abbottabad, Pakistan. But by then, the Al Qaeda movement that Azzam and bin Laden founded had spread into Iraq, Syria, Kurdistan, West Africa, North Africa, sub-Saharan Africa, the Arabian peninsula, Pakistan, India, Bangladesh, Bosnia and Herzegovina, Malaysia, Chechnya, Russia and Spain. Al Qaeda in Iraq has since become known as ISIS, the Islamic State of Iraq and Syria, an even more ruthless and violent extremist organization.

•

IN THE AREAS OF AFGHANISTAN AND PAKISTAN where Taliban extremism is strong, the use of threatening "night letters," and of violence and even murder, to intimidate and silence teachers, administrators and students at girls' schools continues. Yet many courageous people, both male and female, have stepped up to support girls' education. In October 2012 in the mountain province of Swat, just north of Peshawar, a fifteen-year-old girl, Malala Yousafzai, who had gained international attention for speaking out on this issue, was shot in the face by a Taliban gunman as she sat in her school bus. Malala survived, recovered, and continues to speak—in Pakistan and across the world—for the right of all young people to get an education. In 2014 she became the youngest-ever recipient, at age seventeen, of the Nobel Peace Prize.

•

AT THIS WRITING, American and Afghan forces continue to battle the Taliban in Afghanistan. The struggle has become the longest armed conflict in U.S. history.

•

IN THE EARLY 1990s, young Pakistani musicians began to create a hybrid form of music known as "Sufi rock," combining rock 'n' roll with the songs and hymns of the Sufi shrines. By the late nineties, Sufi rock had become hugely popular all over Pakistan. Today, a television program showing live performances of this still-evolving music—often bringing together female pop vocalists with male singers from the shrine culture—draws millions of viewers in Pakistan, while a televised competition among musical performers in Afghanistan, often featuring women, is also hugely popular. These programs, and the music they share, are among the most powerful forces for inclusion and against extremism in these nations today.

DOUG WILHELM is a writer and editor in Weybridge, Vermont. In the early 1980s, he left his newspaper job to spend two years in Pakistan, India and Nepal, traveling, writing, teaching English and working on what he originally planned as a nonfiction book about his experiences, which years later grew into *Street of Storytellers*. Along with *The Revealers,* which continues to be part of the curriculum in middle schools across the country, his previous books include three more young-adult novels, a biography of Alexander the Great for young readers, and 10 books for the Choose Your Own Adventure series. Doug is also a working musician—he plays conga drums, percussion and harmonica in musical groups in Vermont's Champlain Valley.

OTHER BOOKS FROM ROOTSTOCK PUBLISHING

Wave of the Day: Collected Poems
by Mary Elizabeth Winn

Whole Worlds Could Pass Away: Collected Stories
by Rickey Gard Diamond

*Tales of Bialystok: A Jewish Journey from
Czarist Russia to America*
by Charles Zachariah Goldberg

Uncivil Liberties: A Novel
by Bernie Lambek

*Red Scare in the Green Mountains:
Vermont in the McCarthy Era 1946-1960*
by Rick Winston

Fly with A Murder of Crows: A Memoir
by Tuvia Feldman

Lucy Dancer
Story and illustrations by Eva Zimet (Apr. 2019)

Junkyard at No Town
by J.C. Myers (June 2019)

China in Another Time
by Claire Malcolm Lintilhac (Oct. 2019)

The Violin Family
by Melissa Perley, illustrations by Fiona Lee Maclean
(Jan. 2020)